ENDURING GRIT

The Off Grid Survivor Book 3

CONNOR MCCOY

CHAPTER ONE

SARAH LOOKED at the open doorway and thought to herself, with grand fanfare blaring in her mind, *Sarah Sandoval, welcome to your new life.*

She pressed hard on her lower back and gave it a little massage. The bed was softer than the almost-flat mattress she had slept on for the past few weeks, but given the brutal conditions of her captivity, she was thankful for at least something soft to sleep on. *Amazing*, she thought, *to have so much taken away from you, and to now be thankful just to be free.*

Indeed. Before her capture, she had lived in comfort in a high-income suburban neighborhood where she wanted for nothing. Thanks to her boyfriend, she received news of the hottest technical gadgets before much of the population knew about them. One of her favorite tools was the lighting sensors. Whenever she had entered a room in her home, the light snapped on. When she left, the light would wait a few seconds before going out.

She never imagined she lived like a princess until that early morning when the lights went out, and never came back on again.

In a darkened community, Sarah went from a citizen who enjoyed the full perks of society to a desperate survivor. It took a few days to realize the electricity wasn't coming back. She and her boyfriend, Tom Richards, had waited too long to flee the town. By then, the seedier elements of their hometown had risen up and seized their community by the throat.

And then Sarah was captured by a crime boss and hauled away to his warehouse stronghold.

Sarah felt the frame of the dresser mirror before her. The clean glass reflected Sarah's middle-aged image back to her. She tugged at the oversized flannel shirt that hung down to the thighs of her jeans. The outfit wasn't a perfect fit, but few clothes around here were. After all, it's not as if the homestead's owner had anticipated swelling the number of occupants under his roof to six.

And soon to be seven, Sarah thought.

The bright light through the bedroom window almost blinded Sarah as she shuffled away from the mirror. The bed behind her was empty. Tom already had gotten up, got cleaned up and dressed, leaving Sarah to sleep a little longer. Tom easily indulged Sarah in every way, but not just because of love and adoration. He was the reason Sarah was kidnapped in the first place. Love was a powerful motivator, but guilt was sometimes just as strong.

It would have happened anyway, Sarah quickly thought. It was what she told herself to quell any lingering anger she possessed toward Tom. She and Tom had been accosted by a restaurateur named Marco Valentino, who beat Tom and demanded Sarah in exchange for his life. Tom had agreed. Marco rewarded his acquiescence with a blow to Tom's head. At the time, Sarah was sure Tom's skull was cracked. She never imagined she'd see Tom again as she was hauled away to the warehouse of restaurant titan, and now overlord of her hometown, Marcellus Maggiano.

But after a period of captivity, Tom suddenly arrived at Maggiano's warehouse and shot Marco in the chest.

Sarah shook her head. *I want to stop thinking about this*, she thought, and then repeated it a few times. She wanted to get on with her new life.

Her worn brown laced boots stomped down the wooden-paneled floor of the hallway. Then she made a turn through the den, which was really an elaborate workshop filled with tools, books, pamphlets, and little notebooks filled with years of information on everything from basic survival to farming techniques to home construction and maintenance, things Sarah never dreamed she'd have to know.

After walking through this room and unlocking the door on the other side, Sarah emerged on the house's back patio. Rows of crops and livestock pens lay beyond.

There's not a house in sight. I can't see any houses or stores or telephone poles. Sarah's new home was in the country, on this farm. It still rattled her a little. She was not used to horizons that stretched into the distance with no man-made structures in evidence.

On the other hand, this ranch was the most peaceful place she ever had occupied. To be sure, the solar storm had silenced so much of man's modern technology, from its noisy cars to buzzing airplanes, but even so, out here it would be almost as tranquil anyway. This ranch lay off a state road in her home state's countryside, between major metro areas. She never had imagined such tranquility existed.

"Mornin!"

Sarah quivered. Well, not everything around here was peaceful.

Camilla Pitzo looked at her from the other side of a patio post, smiling. Sarah's back arched up. Camilla's smile was one thing Sarah might never get used to. She had no dislike for this woman, but Camilla's mannerisms weren't something Sarah could easily cope with.

"Almost noon, actually," Camilla continued as she approached Sarah, "I know you like to sleep in, but sooner or later you're going to have to spring up with the chickens. Maybe I'll have a rooster bunk out with you. He can give you a wakeup call when you need it."

Sarah grimaced. "Thanks, but I think I'll be okay. I'm ready to get started."

Camilla showed Sarah to the wooden stove a few steps from the house. A table to the right hosted a small mass of clean glass jars. Sliced vegetables and fruits flopped across another table. "They're already cut. Your son brought them by. Can them, heat them up, and we'll be in apricots and carrots for a whole year."

Sarah picked up one of the glass jars. This was her new life, one of a number of new tasks she took up as a farmhand. "I never knew you could can your own food."

Camilla nodded. "I'm sure a lot of people wish they did right now." Then she pointed to the small doors under the stove. "I already took care of the coal and the logs. It's burning right now. Let me know if there's any trouble."

Sarah reached for the two pots on the table that would be used for the canning. Camilla already had filled them with water. Sarah dropped a jar lid into each pot. Then, she placed both pots on the grill. Once the lids were hot enough, she would put them on the jars filled with food, and then put the jars themselves into the pots for additional heating.

And then I take them out and let the heat escape and take out the rest of the air from the jars. Even a dunderhead like me can figure this out, she thought with an inward chuckle.

Just then, movement out the corner of her eye

caught her attention. She turned. An older gentleman was strolling alongside the house, his eyes fixed on the livestock pen out in the field. He and Sarah hadn't spoken yet today. In fact, they rarely did more than exchange some pleasantries.

It's weird when your new home is owned by your ex-husband, Sarah thought. And as Camilla walked away, she mentally added, *and his current girlfriend*.

Indeed, this was a strange new life for Sarah Sandoval.

———

As CONRAD DRAKE approached his sheep pen, he inhaled a deep breath. He felt warm inside. It wasn't everyone who could say he was the master of his own destiny. It was too bad everyone couldn't understand what it felt like.

Only a few clouds dared to interfere with the warmth of the autumn sun. Conrad's land had yielded a strong crop and it was time for harvest. Conrad had grown more than enough for one man to subsist on, but he anticipated he might take on a hired hand or two to help out. Then, when the solar storm struck the Earth's atmosphere and lashed the planet with an EMP, it became clear to Conrad that food and water would be more valuable than gold. Now a large crop became even more useful, as it could be traded for other materials, such as metals or small machine parts. The nearby small towns, having been cut off from regular food shipments, could use all the food they could get.

But that was before his son came knocking on his door with a girlfriend in tow. Before his great adventure to the city of Redmond to rescue his former wife Sarah. Before he met Sarah's boyfriend, Tom, whom he agreed to bring back to the ranch along with Sarah. And finally, before the shootout with a group of men led by a rival rancher named Derrick Wellinger. Thankfully, nobody in Conrad's care was killed, with only a few wounds among the group, bullet holes in the walls, and broken glass to show for their troubles.

The result of the events of those few days was a ranch of six adults. The crops were enough to sustain such a group, but Conrad knew they would have to store up food for the coming winter.

Things had been going well. So well that as Conrad turned to his left and peered at the small hill and the apple tree standing beyond, he began thinking about that special meeting he had planned. He always had found reasons to delay it. He had to bury the bodies of the men who were killed during the battle for his ranch. He had to educate Tom and Sarah in the workings of his home, from how to use the shower to the chores that had to be accomplished. He had to set up the canning process and help Sarah understand what needed to be done, with Camilla helping to instruct her.

But now Conrad could not put it off any longer. It was time for the family reunion.

As Liam approached, pushing a hand dolly holding a bucket of freshly picked cabbages, Conrad saw his chance.

"First load of the day?" Conrad asked as he marched up to his son.

"Second." Liam breathed a little heavy. Sweat poured from under his short dark hair. "Now I know why people get up early on the farm. When it gets around noon, it's like a sauna."

"Well, here's a handy tip. Next time, wear a hat," Conrad said.

Liam rolled his eyes. "Damn. I forgot again."

"These things will start sticking, believe me." Conrad looked over Liam's shoulder. "So, where's the Missus?"

Liam turned around. A lone young female was cutting a cob of corn off one of the stalks. "She's handling the corn. I took care of the cabbage. Tried to find something that didn't require her to bend over so much. I told her to load the corn on the wheelbar-row. I'll take care of it when it's full. No sense in making her haul this stuff inside."

Conrad's eyes darted back to the apple tree. "Look, I think you two ought to wrap things up in the next few minutes."

Liam wiped his forehead. "I know. Lunch is coming up."

"Not just that. We actually have another member

of the family staying here," Conrad said, "Your grandpa, my dad. I didn't have a chance to introduce you."

Liam clung to the dolly even tighter. "Wait, Grandpa is here? Where?" He looked around the farm.

"Easy. He's not inside the house. Bring Carla to the apple tree on that hill in an hour." Conrad pointed to the little spot of land he had been eyeing. "I'll round up Tom, Sarah and Camilla."

———

THE GRAY TOMBSTONE planted in the ground rested in the shadow of the apple tree. The name "James Bradford Drake" was carved on it, along with his birth and death dates. Sandwiched between his dates of birth and death and his name was a phrase: "Father." That was it. No "beloved" father or "loving" father, nothing to qualify the word. To this day, "father" was all Conrad could agree with himself to place on that stone.

Liam knelt down next to the marker and pointed to his grandfather's date of death. "He died last year."

Sarah gazed at the stone with all the ease of a prey animal sensing a predator nearby. Conrad took note of it. He had wondered which of this party would react the worst to this event. Sarah was on the top of his mental list. To be in the presence of his father, even if it was just his bones resting in the ground, would be hard for Sarah.

Carla Emmet kneeled down next to Liam, so close that her curly brunette locks brushed against the left side of Liam's face. "Did you know him well?" she asked, "You never talked about him."

Liam let out a labored breath. "I barely remember him at all. It's just slight flashes in my head, images. I actually remember Uncle Jerry more than Grandpa."

Sarah clutched her arms. "I can't believe he was alive for this long," she said quietly.

Conrad approached her. "I don't think he did, either," he said.

Sarah turned slightly to her former husband. "So, what happened? Did he come here?"

Conrad nodded. "Shortly after the New Year, I got a call from his caretaker. Said that Dad wanted to come by. Now, as you can imagine, having Dad show up is a bit of a scary proposition, so I got some details out of her first." He scratched his upper lip. "Turned out he was harmless, so I said 'sure.' Next day he was driven here."

He tensed up. "Never thought I'd see Dad look that weak. I always remembered him as a force of nature, with hands as big as life. But when he showed up, he looked like death warmed over. A few strokes had taken him down several notches. He couldn't walk. His memory was failing. He couldn't speak but more than a few words at a time."

Sarah's mouth opened a little, while Carla stood up and said, "My God. I'm sorry to hear that."

"Wait, you said his caretaker talked to you?" Sarah said, "What about your brother, Sergeant? Wouldn't he be taking care of your dad?"

"Cirrhosis got Sarge seven years ago. Before that he was in and out of the hospital for five more years. There's no way he could have helped Dad." Conrad glanced at the stone.

"No, Camilla and I took him in. She was living with me at the time. I think Dad knew his time was over and wanted to die in the presence of family." Conrad frowned. "The sad part is we spent our best days together in those last few weeks, only because he had no strength left to fuss or fight over stupid things. I think he also felt guilty that he had outlived Mom and all his sons except for me."

Sarah folded her arms. "Did he ever apologize to you?" she asked, with no amount of disguised resentment. "Did he say a damned thing about the fights he had with you or the way he treated the rest of his family?"

Conrad's eyes met hers. "I think both of us were happy to let sleeping dogs lie," he said, "Besides, I'm not sure he recalled much at all. Some days it was like he was in a dream. He might not have been the best father, but I was not going to cause him any pain by dredging up events that he might not have remembered."

"But it sounds like you two parted on good terms," Tom said. "For what it's worth."

"It was better than I expected." Conrad faced the stone again. For a moment, his voice cracked. "I think...he was even proud of me. I saw it in those eyes on the last day. Couldn't voice a thing, but I'm sure it was there." He sucked in a deep breath. "Personally, I think that's good enough for me."

Liam rose up and stood with Carla. Conrad swallowed. These two youngsters missed out on Grandpa Drake by about a year. How would the old man have reacted if he learned he'd be a great grandfather? How would Liam have reacted reuniting with his grandfather?

Sad part is, once upon a time I wouldn't have wanted Dad and my kid under the same roof, Conrad thought. Perhaps it was all for the best. Conrad's family hardly had been a model family, and many of them had paid for bad living. At least now he could make sure his descendants had a better life.

Conrad turned to Carla and smiled at the young woman. "Four generations of the Drake family on this land. Never imagined such a thing when I built this ranch."

Carla smiled in return while Liam held Sarah's shoulder. "Thanks for showing us Grandpa," Liam said.

Sarah nodded. "Thanks for the news," she said with slight bitterness. Then walked off, not bothering to look at anyone else. "Excuse me, I have more canning to do." Tom quickly ran after her.

Carla's mouth opened. "Is something wrong?" she asked, turning to both Conrad and Liam.

Conrad watched his ex hurry off back to the canning stove. "Don't worry about it, darling. Dad didn't endear himself to Sarah. I hoped this would close a door in her life. Maybe it just reopened an old wound instead."

———

TOM FOLLOWED Sarah closely as she neared her canning stove. Right now following her was like traveling in the wake of a storm cloud. A slight scowl mixed with irritation had plagued Sarah's expression since they had left the hill.

Finally, Tom decided to break the ice, in spite of the old wounds he might be reopening. "Sounds like you had some run ins with Conrad's dad," he said.

Stopping in front of her stove, Sarah sighed. "Him and the whole damn bunch. James, Lacey, Jerry, Sergeant."

"Lacey?" Tom brushed his leg. "That was..."

"Conrad's mom." Sarah raised her head. "She had these eyes, they seemed like they could bore right through you. She never talked much at all. Jerry, oh Lord, he never shut up, and God help you if you got close, he'd grab your arm, slap your back, and his breath was always terrible. He drank and ate the richest food and never cared to chew on a mint if he was in company. He hit on me even when he knew Conrad and I were going out." Sarah put the two pots, which still had water in them, back on the stove.

"Sarge, he was like half Conrad and half James. He had more common sense in him, but he could really blow his stack. It got worse as he got older. It was like his father's blood in him took over." A tremor ran through her body. "I was spooked that the same thing would happen to Conrad."

"I guess I can see why you call them a bunch of hillbillies," Tom said.

Sarah chuckled once as she relit the stove. "Their house, that did it all for me. It was a big house with creaky wooden floors and cracks in the walls, and the whole place had two sections added on to it that never matched. You can thank Jerry for that." She looked away. "The walls also had a few booze stains. The bottles flew in that house. Sometimes when Conrad walked close to the kitchen or the back porch, he'd shake or twitch a little. A lot of the family fights must have gone on there and he'd always remember it."

Tom folded his arms. "Conrad never turned out like his folks. He didn't, right?"

Sarah didn't respond. Tom's skin burned. In the time Tom had spent with Conrad trying to rescue Sarah, he had not witnessed the anger or rage that Sarah had described. But if Conrad hadn't become like his dad, then Sarah might be feeling guilty about leaving him.

What if she regretted it? Did she still harbor feelings for him?

"I believed Conrad would be different from his dad. But then I wasn't sure. I panicked. I imagined all that shouting, the boozing, that it'd be in my house. Any time Conrad and I argued, I pictured his father's face over his." Sarah tensed up. "I didn't give him a chance."

Tom nodded. "What do you think of him now?"

Sarah turned away. "He helped save my life. He gave us a roof to sleep under. What else can I say?"

Tom stepped back, afraid to press any further. For the next few minutes, Sarah continued with her work. Tom figured this would be the right time to slip away.

As he walked back toward the ranch, he wondered what could be churning in Sarah's consciousness right now. The two of the seemed to have made up, but Sarah had not wanted to sleep together since they arrived, which was fine with Tom. As far as Tom was concerned, he owed Sarah a lot and had no desire to pressure her on anything.

Still, he wished he could help Sarah, and right now he wasn't sure he was a help for much of anything.

CHAPTER TWO

THE LIGHT of the candle illuminated Conrad's bedroom mirror, allowing the man to see his own reflection with the slight help of the brightening sky through the window. The time spent at his father's grave yesterday had given him a lot to think about. As he ran his hand through his gray beard, he wondered about shaving it off.

He had worn beards on and off in his young adult years, but when he decided to move out to the city, he had shaved it off completely, thinking he'd fit in better with his urban surroundings. But in time, the clean-shaven face that looked back at him through his bedroom and bathroom mirrors seemed too young, too vulnerable. It didn't reflect who he wanted to be. After moving here about thirty years ago, he let the whiskers grow again.

But reminiscing about the past had stirred old feelings in him. Cutting off the beard seemed to be a way to turn back the clock. Would he look more like his younger self again? Sure, his hair had gone white and gray, but a clean-shaven face still would erase some of the mileage.

An ache then seized his right hand. Wincing, he rubbed his knuckles. Sure, he might look younger, but he wouldn't *feel* younger. The signs of age were catching up with him. Still, he figured he would live perhaps thirty more years or so. After all, his own father had made it into his nineties. Why wouldn't he?

A chill ran across his arm. True, his father lived a long time, but he spent his last few years in degraded health. His caretaker had outlined a steady decline for his father, even before he was hit with his first stroke. He told him of the aches and pains that made it hard for the formerly spry man to walk without a cane and, in the months before the stroke, a walker.

What are you going to do? Conrad thought. *How long are you going to keep up this homestead? Odds are you're not going to keep going at your pace for too much longer.*

The ghosts of the past haunted him. His dad's aged face stared back at him like a phantom in his mirror. His mother then appeared, hair white and limp, before a heart attack claimed her. His brother Jerry was stricken with cancer. And finally, Sarge, who retreated into too many bottles, despite Conrad's entreaties that his brother stop. What would Conrad's end be like?

"Dad!"

Conrad gasped. The phantom vanished from sight. He turned, finding Liam and Carla standing in his open doorway.

"Are you alright?" Carla asked, tilting her head. "You looked like you took a trip to la-la land."

"No kidding," Liam added.

Conrad wiped a bead of sweat off his face. "Oh, just indulging myself in some vanity. Thinking of losing the whiskers. What do you two think?"

Carla laughed. "I don't know. I think you look better with a beard. It's kind of rustic and dignified."

"Dignified, huh?" Conrad stroked his beard. "I like that. So, what's on your minds?"

Liam swallowed. "Carla and I have been talking. We've been wondering if we could go into town and find a doctor. Actually, we don't know if there's one available. We thought you'd know."

"A doctor in town? Not in Hooper City. That's the closest. Why? Are you two feeling okay?"

"Well, it's more like three of us now." Carla patted her stomach. Although she was pregnant, she had yet to show visible signs of the child within her. "And that's what we're concerned about. We'd like somebody to take a look at me. And hopefully, we can have a doctor with us when the time comes for my bundle of joy to make his, or her, appearance."

"There's got to be somebody out there," Liam said. "What about your ham radio? You can call somebody. There's got to be doctors who are helping people."

Conrad cast an eye back to the mirror. As it turned out, he did have somebody in mind. "Don't worry. I know a man who can help us."

"Great," Liam said, "Can you call him in on your radio, or does he live in town? Can we go and get him?"

Conrad smiled. "You don't have to worry about it. I'll fetch him for you."

Carla yawned. "Well, if we've got that taken care of, I still want to help put away our last load of cabbages." She playfully patted Liam on the back before leaving.

Conrad watched her go. Once Carla had walked off, he spoke quietly to Liam. "Busy as a mass of bees, isn't she?"

"She wants to be." Liam yawned. "I think she's just glad to live in a peaceful home. She never takes that for granted."

Conrad understood what Liam meant. Carla's early life wasn't as bad as Conrad's, but Carla still suffered in her formative years, shuttled through the foster system and ending up in the hands of parents who didn't pay much attention to her. She had been forced to steal food until she was taken out of that home and put in the care of an older man who raised her to adulthood. Carla might be a bubbly young lady, but she knew happiness didn't come easy, and sometimes wasn't easily earned.

Conrad stepped around until he faced his boy. "That's good, but you should pull her back a little.

She's not just carrying your kid and my grandchild. She's got the future in her. If she has to put her feet up, let her do it."

Liam sighed. "Neither one of us wants to lounge around when there's work to do."

"Raising the new generation trumps a hand in the field," Conrad said. "Besides, I'm wondering if you got something else on your mind?"

Liam stiffened up. "It sounds like you're going to have to leave to find this doctor. You didn't exactly spill the details."

"Oh, it's no big deal. Doctor Darber actually doesn't live very far from here, but I don't want to cause a big ruckus." Conrad narrowed his eyes. "Look, just don't ask too many questions. If it got out that I had to go, Camilla almost certainly would want to come with me. You've seen how she is whenever my safety's in question."

"I can kind of understand it myself," Liam said, recalling his first conversation with Camilla inside his father's home. Camilla was shaken when Liam and Carla told her they had left Conrad in Redmond to brave Maggiano's men. "For a few days, we didn't know whether you were coming back at all. You could have been killed and we'd never know."

Conrad bowed his head slightly. "I hate that I had to send you away like that. I'm sorry. But we both know it was the right thing to do." He coughed. "Even so, I know it didn't guarantee your safety at all. So, whatever I'll do, I'll do it quickly."

Liam smiled crookedly. "Just tell me you don't have any more personal enemies out there."

Conrad raised an eyebrow. "Enemies? Me? I'm just a humble Midwestern farmer. Who'd have a problem with me?"

"Dad..."

"Trust me, I wish I could tell you. I took Derrick for a hothead, but never a killer and a bandit." Conrad then grasped Liam by the hand. "Don't worry. You've got Tom and Sarah to help defend the home. The odds will be better this time. We've been through the fire. I think we can handle more than we think."

Liam grasped Conrad's hand. "Just try and make it back quickly all the same, please."

Conrad nodded once. "You got my word on that."

———

CONRAD TOOK one more look at the map lying on the drafting table in front of him. The table took up the last bit of space between the wall corner and a small work bench. It was so tightly placed that the table's edges nearly slid against the wall corner on the table's left side.

Conrad finally finished examining the land around the town of South Bend. *If something goes bad on this trip, I could flee toward that river. It's a popular stream, with farmers up and down the line.* He traced the water up the map, stopping near the top. It sounded like a good plan. In the event he lost his bike, or it was damaged, he could flee into the woods near this river and hike upstream to a point just a few miles from State Road 22. Then he stood a good shot of making it back home, provided a band of pursuers didn't cut him off.

"Always have a plan or two," he whispered.

As he rolled up the map, he imagined Sarah's voice in his head. *Conrad, you're the most paranoid person I've ever met on this Earth, except for the guys on the radio. We don't have to worry about losing power for years or months. There's people who always take care of that stuff. Now come on, pull your head out of that stuff, and let's talk about going to Hawaii. For God's sake, I feel like I'm going nowhere in this state. Let's have some fun!*

Conrad finished rolling up his map. He hadn't dreamt of Sarah's voice in a long time. More and more, he expected her to show up in the doorway, commenting on something he was doing, usually aiming a snide or exasperated comment his way.

Conrad was about to leave his workshop when he noticed the cloth-covered load on the small table by the door. He knew what lay underneath, but he couldn't resist a look. He pulled the cloth back, revealing Sarah's jars. She had canned twenty in all for the day. He picked up a jar of apricots and looked at it. Then he gently pressed his thumb on the lid, feeling the concave pit on the center. These jars looked well sealed.

A surge of pride welled up inside him. "We'll

make a frontiersman of you yet, Sarah," he said quietly. "Excuse me, frontierswoman," he added. Canning may not be as difficult as hunting, fishing or growing crops, but it would do as a start. Besides, canning was vital to preserving their food throughout the coming cold months.

I guess now it's all different, Conrad thought. *The Sarah of the past would have thought it crazy to pick up these skills.* He wondered, though, how much Sarah had changed since they parted those years ago. He had not heavily interacted with her since she had arrived here. Sarah would no doubt have her share of mysteries to reveal in the coming days.

He opened up a small plastic case from a work bench, then picked up a few of the jars and set them inside the case. These would be perfect for his errand later on.

The hall floor creaked. Given the night sky outside, Conrad knew who would be up and about. A new routine had set in since the battle with Derrick Wellinger. Conrad, Liam, Carla and Camilla awoke early at sunrise, while Tom and Sarah woke a few hours later. By night, Liam, Carla and Camilla would turn in, while Conrad stayed up longer, and Tom and Sarah would help with keeping watch. Conrad actually hadn't planned this setup. It seemed to have evolved, as Tom and Sarah knew almost nothing about farming life and weren't immediately ready to handle the chores. Besides, Sarah had been through too much of an ordeal for Conrad to push her into daily farming life. He felt canning was a good place to start for her.

Conrad opened the door. Indeed, Sarah was out there, wearing a belt with a sidearm snug in a holster. She also was carrying a shotgun. Conrad's eyes widened. This was not a sight he'd have imagined, not while he was married to her, and certainly not in the years while they were separated. Conrad hadn't even asked her to keep watch. Tom volunteered, and Sarah then asked to help him. At first Conrad suspected Sarah just wanted to be by her man's side, but lately he got the feeling she was truly into this.

I wondered how much she changed? Conrad thought. *Seems like she changed a lot.*

"You're up late, even for you," Sarah said.

"Just doing some land research. Keeping some local details in the old noggin." He tapped his forehead. "So, what's your story?"

"Tom and I are going to take a look at the fence," she replied. "He's putting in the solar batteries for the flashlights. Shouldn't be long."

"I'll stay up until you two get back inside. Don't forget to turn in soon. I don't want you two to turn into night owls and stumble around like zombies in the daytime."

"Says you." Sarah smirked. "You never go to bed before anyone else. Maybe Tom and I will push you and see if you still get your bones out of bed before six in the morning."

"You know I'm not a heavy sleeper," Conrad said.

"Well, I know you weren't." Sarah bit her lip. "It's been a long time. We kind of got old since then."

Conrad chuckled. "Hey, I was still a few years off from collecting Social Security before the world got its lights shut off. So, I hadn't crossed that line yet."

"Makes me feel stupid for paying payroll taxes all those years," Tom said as he crossed into the living room from the kitchen. Then he nodded to Sarah. "The lights are ready."

Sarah started walking toward Tom. "Thanks." Then she addressed Conrad as she followed Tom through the kitchen. "You don't have to wait up. I'll lock it all down when I'm done."

Conrad watched her leave, listening to the loud thumps of her boots. No doubt about it. Serving as security for the homestead had filled Sarah with vigor. Perhaps it was just the motherly instinct to protect her son and her grandchild?

She doesn't want to be a victim anymore, he thought. That might be it. If she ever was accosted again, she didn't want to be helpless. The next time, her would-be abductors would take a bullet in the chest and head before they took her.

Also, Conrad couldn't help but bristle when Tom came in. Was Conrad feeling jealous? No, that couldn't be it. There was nothing between him and Sarah except the desire to protect their offspring, even if they were no longer husband and wife. In the time since, they had grown too far apart for any reconciliation to occur. Besides, Conrad and Sarah each had new significant others.

But neither one of us remarried, Conrad thought. Perhaps that was a sign that it wasn't truly over.

"Damn it all, Conrad," he whispered to himself, "Stop wrestling with old phantoms and get with it."

He angrily cursed himself out in his head as he walked to his bedroom. There was more work to be done, and he had to do it quickly before he went to sleep. He had an early rise tomorrow—earlier than usual.

CHAPTER THREE

"Easy, son," Ronald Darber said as the young man stumbled up Darber's porch steps, with the soft rays of the morning sun bouncing off the youngster's back. Darber dashed across the porch and made it to the box in the courier's hands before it slipped completely from his grasp. Darber took hold of it and then carried the load through his front door.

"Come in and sit down," Darber said, "Good lord, don't they ever feed you?"

The young man shuffled inside, doubled over. He was so out of it that Darber feared the man would collapse on his floor. Darber took hold of his guest by his right arm and helped him to an easy chair in the Darber living room. Fortunately, the house was small, with the living room, kitchen, and small physician's office all easily accessible within several steps. A soft breeze blew through the window screens. The man moaned loudly before plopping down in the soft seat.

Darber took a quick look in the box. Fruits, vegetables, and a bottle of water. The rations came as promised. So, Kurt was pleased with Darber this week. Darber let out a contented sigh. Four times in the past, he accidentally had irritated Kurt over something, perhaps a misspoken word or a facial expression that seemed to Kurt like a scowl or a sneer, although Darber meant no disrespect. In response, Kurt would delay the rations by a day or so as a way to toy with him. Kurt was a complicated fellow. Most of the time he never let on when he was being slighted, or thought he was being slighted.

When Kurt did let someone know they had offended him, it wasn't pleasant. Not at all.

Darber learned pretty quickly what to tell Kurt and what not to. Kurt never tolerated lying, but on the other hand, he didn't appreciate bluntness. So, Darber made sure to massage his words as carefully as possible. He could tell him bad news, he just had to say it along with mentioning the possibility of a solution down the road. It worked this week. But it might not next.

So, once again, he would conserve his rations carefully, to make them last as long as they could. Fortunately, Darber understood how much the human body required to keep going. Water was essential. He would drink that in small doses throughout the upcoming week. He'd also be aware of dizzy spells. An empty stomach and too much work could cause an ill feeling that Darber would like to avoid. As he recently had turned fifty-four, he was more aware of his limitations than ever, and knew not to overwork himself.

The courier wheezed a little. Darber shook his head. The youngster was skinny, with his clothes hanging loose from his body. He seemed to wear the same oversized red shorts and dirty blue shirt, and more than once his shorts fell off him completely. The courier could be fresh out of high school. Darber wasn't sure, for the doctor never asked him his age. Actually, Darber didn't know much about him, except for his name. What was it again?

"Lance?" Darber asked as he pulled out a small paper cup from his kitchen cabinet. Then he poured some water from his bottle into the cup and offered the small portion to Lance. The young courier took the cup and downed it quickly. "I hope that's the last haul for you this morning," Darber added.

Lance coughed. "Thanks. I-I got to go. I get chewed out if I don't get back before seven."

"You'd think they give you a bicycle at least to ride around town," Darber said.

"They say I got to earn it." Lance coughed again. "They said I should be glad I get to sleep in the attic at Tony's."

Darber rolled his eyes. "How generous."

Lance got up. Actually, he climbed up, using the armrests as leverage to pull his body to a standing position. He wobbled, but after a moment his body steadied itself. Darber winced when he noticed how sunken-in Lance's eyes were. The kid clearly had lost a lot of weight quickly.

"Oh," Lance said weakly, "Kurt says he'll be by tomorrow. He wanted you to check his, uh, his..."

A chill ran down Darber's back at the notion of Kurt coming by, but he pushed it aside. "Probably wants me to test his reflexes and pain responses. Did he say anything about the alcohol I requested?

Lance shook his head. "Naah. Not a word. I didn't ask. You know I can't."

"Yes, yes, you're right." Darber's face tightened. The mere act of asking for something was an almost sure way to get a smack in the face. Darber was amazed that he managed to broach such a subject with Kurt and not invite retribution. Kurt even seemed amused at the time.

I'm nothing more than a house pet to him, Darber thought.

Lance hurried for the door. "I'll see ya tomorrow," he said. He almost tripped twice, but made it out the door, across the porch, and onto the side street that stretched out into the neighborhood, without incident.

Darber strolled onto his porch. "Godspeed," he muttered half-jokingly as Lance disappeared around a street corner. Even a short walk across a few blocks had become like an epic journey. If the people here received proper nourishment and medicine, the new world wouldn't be such an ordeal. But when the wrong people are in charge, all of a sudden resources

become tightly controlled. Now you owe your exis-
tence to someone else, and if you're of no value,
you're expendable.

Ronald Darber was damn lucky he was a doctor.
The new rulers in town prized his skills and gave him
the provisions needed to survive. That was the only
currency that mattered now. Paper money and coins
were laughed at. If you had food and drink, you were
a king. No, even a god to some people. People such as
Kurt.

Darber plodded back into his small home, which
doubled as his office. He might have lived in a
Midwestern state with many farms, but he was no
rancher or farmer. He understood the innards and
operations of the human body, but couldn't fathom
how to successfully till a garden. Like so many others,
he took modern conveniences for granted. He never
dreamed one day they would not be available.

That's why I'm stuck, Darber thought. Sure, he
could leave town. He even kept a bicycle hidden away
in a home closet. Unfortunately, he didn't possess the
food or supplies for a long journey, or even a short
one. If he tried to gather supplies, he'd draw suspi-
cion, and then any window of freedom he had would
be gone. They'd always be looking in on him. They
might even confine him to his house.

He turned his eye back to his kitchen. Better to
enjoy the solitude while he had it. Kurt would come
calling tomorrow.

———

PERCHED ON HIS BICYCLE, Conrad's heart sank as he gazed upon the first few homes that made up what was going to be a lovely suburb. For well over a hundred years, Davies was a set of homesteads and dusty roads, a tiny dot on the map that few ever paid attention to. But time brought expansion of the towns to the north, all the way to the borders of Davies. And so, this tiny little backwater, over the past two decades, had been transforming into a suburb.

But now that expansion was stopped dead in its tracks. Houses that were under construction now were frozen in a state of partial completeness. Wooden frames formed skeletons of homes that would not be finished. Some workers had managed to put up drywall before the solar event hit. One or two homes possessed roofs, but the shingles had not been added.

A nice comfy suburb, with no farms or livestock in sight. God only knew what these people must have thought when the modern world shut down around them. Did they all flee to the countryside in the hope of finding food? Or did they hunker down here? If it was the latter, there must be a supply line to send them food. After all the time that passed since the EMP, there's no way anyone could survive here without regular provisions.

One way Conrad could find out would be to ask a

local. But for the past twenty minutes, he hadn't found so much as a soul on these streets.

As the flock of new homes gave way to older, completed structures, he began noticing something else. The cars, trucks, any automobile he passed, whether in a driveway or stalled on a curb, had their gas tank covers opened. Conrad slowed down as he approached a small red car on the side of the road. The gasoline tank cover yawned open.

They've been taking fuel out of the cars, Conrad thought. It made sense. There might be a few generators in town that still were functional and could run off gasoline. Cannibalizing the gasoline from vehicles that wouldn't start up anyway was a smart move. Even so, Conrad wished there was somebody around to ask.

Additionally, this town wasn't as messed up as Conrad had expected. Sure, the lawns were overgrown, with nobody having tended to them in weeks. And, of course, vehicles lay around completely stalled, with no way to start them up. But the streets themselves were quite clean for a town whose regular garbage service abruptly had ceased. There were leaves, twigs, but little man-made trash.

There were also no dead bodies. In the event of a societal catastrophe where systems broke down, people could expire on the street due to hunger, thirst, disease, or attacks from feral animals. One of the great apocalyptic horrors of urban areas was the accumulation of corpses. But that wasn't the case here.

Once you've secured provisions, one of the first orders of survival after a catastrophe is getting diseases and infections under control, Conrad thought. It was just like what happened in Redmond with Maggiano's empire. Dead bodies and feces were magnets for viruses and bacteria. Maggiano wanted to rule that town, but there would be no point in ruling a town infested with disease. So, he enlisted survivors to haul away human and animal carcasses.

"So, who's in charge here?" he asked the wind.

Conrad's bike soon approached the intersection of the oldest part of town. Suddenly, a pungent odor grabbed hold of his nostrils. Was that smoke? He inhaled more deeply. No, that was more like exhaust. Vehicle exhaust. It may have been over a month since he was in a world with working automobiles, but it was hard to forget such a smell.

Now Conrad was suspicious, more than usual. A working car or truck? Who around here possessed one?

He pedaled harder down the street. Sure enough, up ahead in the distance he spotted something turning. It was big, too big to be moved by human hands or to be pulled by horses. It looked like an automobile. It was too large to be a car. Maybe it was a van. No, Conrad had caught a glimpse of the rear window and the shape of the cab around it. There also seemed to be a truck bed just behind the window. All of the details added up to a large pickup truck.

But as fast as Conrad could pedal, he couldn't reach the street corner in time. The vehicle had made its turn, and it was a good few minutes before Conrad had reached the intersection. By the time Conrad turned his bike onto the road, there was no truck present.

Conrad inhaled. There was definitely fresh exhaust in the air. His mind wasn't playing tricks on him. Then he looked down to the asphalt. A few pieces of garbage—aluminum cans, mangled cardboard—all were flattened. Tire treads even were pressed onto an old fast food container.

Conrad pushed on his pedals again. He was determined to track down the mystery truck.

But a half an hour later, fatigue gripped him, and he had to stop on a curbside. He had been pedaling a lot today, with few breaks. Now his sudden mystery truck hunt had sapped even more of his energy.

"Dammit Conrad, you're losing focus here." He had come to Davies to find Doctor Darber, but instead he had latched on this enigma like a dog to a bone.

He wiped his forehead with his sleeve. A still-working vehicle shouldn't be that unusual. An EMP blast would fry electronics installed in automobiles, but not every vehicle possessed such wiring and circuitry. Older vehicles could escape the assault of an electromagnetic pulse and still work, provided they had gas, oil and a working battery.

So maybe the gas around here isn't being siphoned for a generator. It could be for that truck, Conrad thought.

After a few minutes, Conrad mounted his bicycle again. First thing's first. Doctor Ronald Darber should be his top priority. Besides, Conrad could ask the doctor what's going on.

———

LANCE CARRIED his latest load down the street, his long light brown hair dangling in front of his face. He had recovered enough of his strength to carry this box to his latest recipient, an auto worker named Juan. He just hoped he could make it to Juan's auto repair shop before he collapsed again from exhaustion.

When are these guys going to up my food ration? Lance blew another lock of hair from his face. *And how about a decent haircut? Or at least a pair of scissors?*

As he passed a line of houses, a figure on a bicycle sped past, pedaling down the street. In an instant, Lance glimpsed the figure and was so startled he dropped his box onto the sidewalk.

No, not him!

Lance quaked. No, his eyes had to be playing a trick on him. Conrad Drake, the man who had chased him off his property with a freakin' hand grenade! No, he couldn't have just pedaled by on a bike.

Bad memories flooded into his mind with the force of water bursting from a dam. Phantom sounds of gunfire shook him down to his feet. He recalled the shots of the men around him, and the bullets spitting back at them from the ranch, some of which struck men down around him. Then, he and one other man had fled the property, with Conrad lobbing hand grenades behind them. Like the other men who had joined Derrick Wellinger, he was looking for a job in exchange for food and shelter. But in the end, Lance survived only to be left with nothing.

Then he wandered about the state roads, so hungry that at one point he was reduced to eating grass to survive. Before long, his travels took him to a nearby town, and then here to Davies, where the promise of food and shelter attracted him.

So, why the hell did that nightmare follow him all the way here?

Lance scooped up the box. He had to make this delivery to Juan. Hopefully, this was all a bad daydream, and he'd never see that man again, ever.

————

RONALD DARBER'S eyes snapped open. Who was that?

He looked down the road. The wind had brushed

against the loose siding of a nearby store. Darber clutched his chest. He had fallen asleep again in his porch chair, once again at the mercy of the outdoor sounds.

He clutched the banister of his porch. He should get inside. If he wasn't so haggard, he'd have thought to go back into his house earlier, before he took an unexpected nap. He had no business sleeping out here, where he was noticeable and vulnerable.

Damn, Darber thought as he rubbed his eyes. *You overworked yourself again today*.

The sun was starting to set. Darber's legs twitched. Now he had even more reason to go inside. Kurt had brought a lot of order to Davies, but even so, it's not like his men patrolled the streets at night like evening security guards or policemen.

But before he could turn back to his front door, a lone figure approached on a bicycle from the street that ran past his home. His heart quickened. For a moment he feared the worst, perhaps a messenger from Kurt with bad news, or even Kurt himself arriving early. Yet, as the man on the bike came closer, Darber noticed the rider's disheveled white hair and beard. This was an older man, not anybody Darber recognized from around town.

Darber leaned over the banister. No, he knew that man. "Conrad!" he called out.

Conrad slowed his bike and soon stopped it short of the Darber home's porch steps. Conrad then let out a long breath, followed by a cough. "Damn," Conrad muttered, "the miles sure catch up with you."

Darber quickly ran down the steps. "You look worse every time I see you," Darber said with a chuckle.

Conrad looked down at his friend. Darber's height was about a foot shorter than Conrad's six-foot-tall frame. "Always knew your eyesight would go one day."

Darber laughed. "I'm going to have to let you have that one." He took Conrad by his right hand and shook it. "So, what brings you here, besides the end of the world?"

Conrad looked around thoughtfully. "As it turns out, I don't know much about childbirth. Thought I'd consult an expert."

Darber's eyes widened. "Camilla? Conrad, good lord..."

Conrad laughed. "No, it's not Camilla. Someone different. She's my son's girl, and she needs to be checked over. I need you to come back with me. I know it may be asking a lot, but I'd also like to have you there when she delivers."

"That's what I love about you, Conrad. You get right to the point." Though Darber chuckled as he said it, he was grateful Conrad was spilling his story so quickly. Better yet, Conrad's offer was a godsend. Still, Darber couldn't let on how intensely he was interested in Conrad's request.

Darber walked up the porch steps. Conrad

followed. "Yeah, I wish I could do the whole 'catch up on old times' routine, but I've had some trouble at the homestead," Conrad said. "Another homesteader thought he could grab my property by force. It was nasty. Fortunately, nobody in my care was killed, but there were some injuries. I wasn't there for much of it, and I want to speed this up so I'm not away from home too long."

Darber didn't like the sound of Conrad's story. "But it's safe now, right?"

"I got some additional help to guard the home, including my ex. But there's no immediate danger that I know of."

That was good enough for Darber. "That's great. I'm glad you didn't lose anyone. It's not everyone who can say that nowadays."

"Yeah." Conrad raised an eyebrow. "Sounds like you've heard of some trouble yourself. Anything going on in Davies?"

Darber's skin burned. "Well, you hear all kinds of things. But enough about that. You say you need a doctor."

"I do. I hate to pull you away from Davies. Are you in the middle of treating anyone? We can work out something."

"No, no!" Darber backed up against his living room's rear wall. "No, actually, a lot of people have fled Davies, so my patient pool isn't what it used to be. I'm open for whatever you need, even if you want a long stay."

"You sure about that? I figured you're still eating good, so I imagine your patients must be trading you food for service."

"Yes, you could say that," Darber replied.

"Well, you can count on a lot more at my ranch," Conrad said. "I'll give you food, water, and some other resources if you need them, metals, building wood. I've also grown some herbs on my ranch that are helpful for medicine."

Darber smiled slightly. "Well, who can say no to that? Consider it a deal." He turned to the hallway. "I'll get packing immediately."

Conrad watched Darber move about the house. The doctor pulled out an old, worn brown leather suitcase and flung it open. Darber packed up clothes and supplies with such speed that it seemed as though he was both exhilarated and scared out of his wits all at once.

"Ron, you okay?" Conrad finally asked, "You're moving like your ass is on fire."

Darber looked up from his case. "I suppose I'm just excited for you." He smiled, a little unconvincingly. "I'd like to leave before sunset. You do have camping equipment on you, right?"

"Sure. Got a nice tent, can house us for the night, but why not bunk out here? I don't wish to impose, but we're not in an awful hurry." Conrad almost laughed. He never thought he'd be the one to slow things down.

Darber exhaled softly. "I'd like to get started as

soon as possible if you could. I think it would be a bit difficult to linger here longer than I have to."

Conrad nodded. "Okay. All due speed it is. If you need any help –"

"I'm fine." Darber looked to his office. "Don't worry. I'll be ready to go in just a few minutes."

CHAPTER FOUR

SARAH YAWNED. Another day of canning awaited her. *It helps finally to have a job of some kind*, she thought. Before too much longer, this life might actually feel normal to her.

She pulled the pajamas from her skin. Given how tight they were, she only could muster about an inch. Carla had been generous in loaning her these, although the fact that Carla's stomach was beginning to expand helped. Soon Carla wouldn't fit well in many of her regular clothes.

Sarah's skin tingled at the thought. A grandbaby! It was amazing to behold.

Glimpsing herself in a hall mirror, she took note of her dark hair, now graying, and thought to herself, *You're definitely older now. Time to admit it*. She had kept herself in good shape these past few decades, but she had to admit her energy had flagged a little. She had to stretch a little more in bed before she felt ready to take on the day. Sarah even recalled Conrad checking out his beard in a mirror recently.

I know he's thinking the same thing, she added.

She rounded the hallway corner, stepping into the dining room. She looked to the door leading to the living room and then to the side door leading outside, expecting Conrad to walk by and mutter his customary hello. Instead, both the kitchen and dining room were quiet. A folded note on the dining room table marked with a cursive "Sarah" greeted her.

She picked it up and unfolded it. No doubt about it, this was Conrad's handwriting—and rather bad writing, too. Picking her way through the words was a chore, but after a couple of read-throughs she got the gist of it. Conrad had left the house early to travel to a small suburb named Davies, where he would find and pick up a Doctor Ronald Darber. He should be back in about two days.

"'Remember, there's always work to be done,'" Sarah read. She stopped to roll her eyes. "You've drilled that into our heads several times over, but hey, once more on paper couldn't hurt," she remarked before reading again, "'And always keep a gun on you, especially when you're outside, just in case.'"

Lowering the paper from her eyes, Sarah sighed and sank back against the wall. "No rest for the weary, right Conrad?"

A set of footsteps drew her attention. Tom was

standing in the hall, all dressed up, with fresh sweat rolling down his face. "Talking to Conrad?"

Sarah pushed the paper into his chest. "He left. Only for a couple of days. It's all in here." Tom took it. "You need me to translate any of it?" Sarah asked.

Tom blinked his eyes as he studied the paper. "I hope he never had to write post-it notes for you while you were married."

Sarah helped Tom along, eventually reading just about all of the letter. Soon Tom had gotten the full story. "I guess he couldn't trouble us with a goodbye," he said. He clutched the paper hard.

"I guess some things never change," Sarah said. "Conrad was always a little paranoid."

"I think the prepped house and ranch pretty much confirms that," Tom said.

"It's not just that." Sarah stretched her arms. "It was little things. He couldn't relax. It was always hard to get what he was thinking out of him. He didn't share thoughts easily."

Tom nodded. "Always played it too close to the vest."

Sarah nodded. "Yeah."

Tom folded up the letter. "I better make sure Camilla and the kids know."

Sarah raised an eyebrow. "The kids?"

Tom chuckled. "Liam and Carla."

"Dear Lord," Sarah said, "I guess we're both getting older." She ran her left hand through Tom's hair above his left ear. "I'm starting to see some silver in there."

Tom licked the insides of his mouth. "It's the sun. It's definitely the sun." He tilted his head toward the sunlight pouring through the nearby window.

Sarah laughed. "Hey, whatever makes you rest easy, but sooner or later the mirror won't lie." Then she stretched again. "I'd better get started with more canning."

————

DARBER SIPPED THE SOUP. "This is good." He looked up. "Rice and meat. Never had that combination before."

Conrad looked down at his own cup. "It's called gumbo. It's popular in Louisiana. Usually you pop in rice and sausage, but I like to chop up the meat a little more. I don't like making the sausages too big."

Conrad had pitched a tent in the shadow of an old oak tree off the side of the road. In this darkness it would be impossible to spot them. Someone would have to get off the road and hike here, then turn to the side with a good light to illuminate their campsite.

Conrad watched Darber as he ate. Every now and then the doctor would crane his head back in the direction of the road.

"So how's Tara?" Conrad asked.

"Tara?" Darber asked.

Conrad smiled. "Now don't tell me you forget about her already."

Darber shook his head. "Sorry. I suppose my head's in another place. I haven't seen her in weeks. But we've been doing well. Our last visit went fine, but she had to return to her family in Staples. She has an ill sister and an aging mother. Pulling the plug on the world has had sad consequences for so many. And what about you and Camilla?"

"Back at the ranch. She's probably there to stay," Conrad replied.

A slight smile formed on Darber's face. "Considering another try at the altar?"

"Now that's a terrible thing to suggest, Doctor. When a man is let out of jail, you don't just walk back in."

Darber laughed so hard he started coughing. "Good lord, Conrad. I hope you're not that soured on the idea of getting hitched."

Conrad smiled at his own joke. "Well, the truth is there's still some hard feelings that haven't died yet. It's only in the last few months that I can think of it without getting a pain in my stomach." He scratched his right fist. "I still don't know if I can ever be the man who stays in the valley."

"Stays in the valley?" Darber asked.

Conrad shrugged. "Forget about it. Silly talk. Anyway, I have something I've been dying to ask you. When I came into Davies, I could have sworn I saw a pickup truck going through town. Someone actually was driving it. I smelled the exhaust, saw the tire treads, just about everything. Now, I know the EMP from the sun didn't fry every vehicle on the planet, but it's still pretty surprising to see a truck running. Do you know anything about it?"

Darber scratched his left ear while looking away. "Someone does have a working truck in town. The town currently has some new bosses. They gathered up a couple of trucks, but they don't use them very much. You know that the gas stations don't work, and it's not like we'll be getting new shipments soon."

"But they must have siphoned from just about every vehicle in Davies," Conrad said, "I saw a lot of cars with their fuel tanks open."

Darber nodded. "It's not as if anyone else needs it."

"Perhaps someone has a working generator," Conrad said.

"If they do, I don't know about it," Darber said a little gruffly.

Conrad bristled. They had left town too quickly for his tastes, and now he couldn't investigate the mystery truck he had spotted. Darber's answers didn't help. They were too vague and dodgy. This man wanted out of Davies, but he never had said why. And who were these new bosses Darber spoke of?

"Just as long as things are going well back home," Conrad said, and he watched Darber closely to see how he reacted.

The doctor nodded. "Of course," he said.

After a short while, Darber decided to turn in. For his part, Conrad stayed up and kept watch over the stars.

Perhaps I'm fussing over nothing, Conrad thought. It was hard to imagine just about any community could be a place worth living in. The loss of power and the destruction of so much electronic equipment had turned so many hometowns into ugly places. Just about everybody probably wanted to be somewhere else. So, why not Ronald Darber? And even if something was going wrong in Davies, was it really Conrad's problem? Besides, Darber was able to leave. It wasn't as if someone tried stopping them at gunpoint.

Unless leaving quickly threw someone off Darber's trail, Conrad thought to himself.

Conrad wrestled with his doubts a little longer before he fell asleep. Even so, he wondered again if he was the man who could stay in the valley.

The man in the valley, he thought. *The man who could have a home.*

———

LANCE, sound asleep, was dreaming of happier times, when he had a functioning air conditioner blowing in his face, could hang out with friends, chow down on a big cheeseburger with pickles and onions, listen to music on his phone, speed his car along the old dirt roads that ran behind small towns, and even see his parents again.

He trembled a bit as his dreams turned to his folks. The last time he saw them was just before the solar storm struck. They were headed off to Florida on a vacation to Miami Beach. Their budget couldn't afford Hawaii, so Florida was the next best thing. They hopped on a plane for a week-long vacation.

The next day, the whole world shut down.

Lance had no hope of flying from his Midwestern perch down to Florida, nor could his parents return here on an airplane, a train or even a rented automobile. They were trapped in a state with millions of people. Lance was told by a farmer that his parents were caught up in one of the worst outcomes, to be ensnared in a densely packed area with no power, and that he shouldn't get his hopes up of seeing them again. The riots and upheaval would make escaping from southern Florida almost impossible.

Lance admitted he wasn't all that close to his parents, but he hardly hated them either. And right now, if he was with them again, it'd be enough.

But whatever else Lance could imagine in his dreams was interrupted when a large, hairy hand seized him by his shirt and pulled him into a sitting position. "Get up!" roared a voice carried by hot breath.

Lance's eyes shot open. "What? What?" When he saw he was nearly nose to nose with Vander, he screamed.

Vander responded by shaking Lance like a doll. "Shut it. You're coming with me."

Lance was dragged through the attic where he slept, passing by two other men who likely already were awake from the commotion, but feigning sleep to avoid drawing attention. Vander didn't allow Lance to walk under his power. The six-foot-tall, red-haired man hauled the young man to the open steps. "Now climb down!" Vance ordered, spit flying from his mouth.

Lance scrambled down the steps to the second floor below. The building that Lance called home was a run-down old store called Tony's Furniture. The place was two stories tall with and an attic that would be stifling if holes weren't cut into the sides and the stairwell wasn't always down. Unfortunately, the attic also leaked when it rained, but Lance's benefactors had no interest in repairing it. By this point, Lance counted himself lucky that he had a home at all, and wasn't sleeping in a ditch.

Vander joined Lance, then grabbed him again, this time by the back of his shirt, and hauled him down the hall to a small room. Another man, Blake, awaited him inside. The dawning sky clearly was visible in the window behind him.

Vander shoved Lance through the door, enough that Lance fell flat on his stomach onto the hard floor. "The doc's gone," Vander said.

Lance coughed as he sat up. "Doc?"

"Darber, you moron." Blake took a step closer, his

dirty boot thumping the floor so hard and suddenly that it rattled Lance's ears.

Blake was shorter than Vander, but then again just about everyone around here was dwarfed by the brute. However, Blake was no less ruthless when he wanted to be. Blake was just smoother about it, the guy that would jab a knife in your back rather than smash your face in with a fist.

"He's gone," Blake said, "Split. He packed up, so he knew he was going. You were the last guy to see him."

Vander hovered right over Lance. "So, what was the deal with the doc?" Vander asked. "Did he tell you where he was going?"

"What? No-no, he didn't say he was going anywhere!" Lance said, sweat dripping down his face.

"He didn't tell you a goddamn thing?" Blake didn't sound at all like he believed Lance.

"He was just doing his same old stuff, nothing different!" Lance blurted out. "I gave him his rations like I'm supposed to, and then I left! That's all!"

Vander walked, very slowly, around Lance. "You're going to have to give us more than that. He's Kurt's doctor. Kurt isn't happy that his doctor isn't around. So you better cough up something—fast."

Lance hyperventilated. *Okay, think! Think! What can I tell these guys? Wait, Conrad! Yeah, maybe it's all his fault!*

"Um, wait! Conrad! Yeah, I saw him in town just as I left!" Lance said quickly.

"Conrad?" Blake sneered. "Who the hell is Conrad?"

Lance spread his arms. "Okay, he's this old rancher who lives somewhere north of here. It'd be a day away on a bike. Anyway, I used to work for Derrick Wellinger. Derrick pulled us together and we were going to kick Conrad off his land." He trembled. "He's a scary son of a bitch. He tried to blow me away with a hand grenade!"

"A hand grenade?" Blake raised an eyebrow. "Who is this guy, an ex-military?"

"I don't know who he is!" Lance cried out, "But he was here in town, and I'm sure he was going to see Darber." That last part was a lie, but Lance had to feed these guys something in the hope they'd let him go.

"Conrad." Blake's eyes met Vander's. "Doesn't sound like anybody that's from around here."

Vander turned back to Lance. "So, where does Conrad live?"

"I'll tell you!" Lance said. By aiming these animals at Conrad Drake, these two would have something else to chew on and leave him alone.

Blake raised a hand. "Better yet, he's taking us there."

Lance fell back on his posterior. "What?"

"You heard him." Vander backed up toward the door. "You're leading us to this Conrad's house. Then we'll see if you're telling us the truth."

"But I don't want to go back there!" Lance yelped,

"He's a monster! He's nuts! A psycho! He'll blow us away in a minute!"

Blake cracked his knuckles. "You worried about this Conrad guy icing you? Better to worry about what Kurt will do to you. If you don't help us get his doctor back, you'll be planted head first into the ground."

CHAPTER FIVE

DARBER'S BREATHS grew heavier as Conrad led them closer to the turnoff. Conrad slowed up so he could ride parallel with the doctor. "Ready for a rest yet?"

"Yes..." Darber let out a long breath as he reduced his speed. "I figured all the weight I lost in the past few weeks would whip me into better shape."

"It's the muscles, doctor. Being as thin as a nail means you're as strong as one," Conrad said.

Darber's bike nearly tipped over. "Whoa." Conrad pulled in a little closer. "You better bring that to a stop. You look like you're going to faint in a mud puddle."

"I'm sorry." Darber halted his bike. Then he climbed off and held onto his ride for a few minutes. Conrad stopped as well, gazing at his friend as the doctor tried getting his bearings.

"You sure were in a hurry to get going. You didn't

even accept my offer to rest a few miles back," Conrad said.

"I know." Darber stared at the road behind them. "I just...I just wanted to get going for your grand-child's sake."

"Well, you won't be any good to my family if you're too worn out to help." Conrad scratched the back of his neck. Darber definitely was jittery about something.

After a few more minutes' rest, Conrad led Darber to the road that turned off from State Road 22. "Now, this is the main road that goes into Hooper City. We might as well take a breather here, plus I got something for one of the merchants here."

As Conrad finished speaking, a lone figure on a red bicycle pedaled up to them from the turnoff, emerging from the row of houses just ahead.

"And, speaking of which..." Conrad stopped. "Nigel! Good Lord, talk about good luck that you're in the neighborhood!"

Nigel stopped and put down his bike's kickstand. "Our sentry spotted you two come in and passed the word along."

"Sentry?" Conrad walked over and shook Nigel's hand. "Now that's a change. Oh doctor, this is Nigel Crane, owner of the finest feed store in Hooper City."

"Doctor, huh?" Nigel turned to Darber. "Where'd Conrad dig you up?"

"Davies," Darber said, a little nervously.

"Davies? Haven't heard any news out of there lately," Nigel replied. "Well, Conrad, you're pretty lucky to find a doc at all. We had to send three sick people off to Salinger's farm. That was about a six-hour journey, but it was the best we could do."

"Nothing will be easy for a long time." Conrad said, shaking his head. "But, I do have something that will help. I come bearing..." He pulled out a jar of carrots. "...a gift." He handed it to Nigel. "Now, that baby's vacuum-sealed and will last for about two years if necessary. I wish I had more on me, but I had to make a trip to bring the doctor here to my home. About to have the pitter-patter of little feet in my home, if you get my drift."

"Yes, I remember you told me." Nigel grinned as he turned the jar upside down and right side up again. "We've got so many people in town who don't know how to preserve food this good."

"I'm telling you, it's not hard. Did you gather all the glass jars like I asked you to?"

Nigel nodded. "Sure...sure..."

Conrad frowned. Nigel wasn't looking at him, and the store owner's words seemed slower than usual. "Now you look like you're head's in another place, Nigel. What's going on?"

Nigel lowered the jar from his face. "We've had another run in with bandits. The same two. At least this time we had guards around the storehouse. They didn't get anything." Nigel sighed. "But we got a good look at one of them. He was definitely one of Derrick Wellinger's men."

"Damn," Conrad said, "Even in death the man's legacy is a cancer around here."

"Wellinger?" Darber turned to Conrad. "He's the guy who tried to kill you and steal your ranch, right?"

"Yeah." Conrad's face tightened. "Some of his cohorts got away. I was hoping they'd turn over a new leaf, but it seems some of them aren't going to learn shit until someone puts a bullet in their head. We got word that one of them has been stealing crops in Hooper City. They're probably desperate. They don't know where their next meal is coming from, so they'll take it at the point of a gun."

"Conrad, I think you should stay away from town for a few days. It's not exactly safe to conduct big trades in the open," Nigel said. "Give us a chance to get the guards into shape. If you show up with more cans, you never know if these lunatics will jump you."

"It's alright," Conrad replied. "We need more time anyway to can more crops. Look, why don't you come by with some empty jars. We'll trade some extra crops for more metal and wiring."

"I appreciate it." Nigel offered his hand. "Be careful out there."

Conrad took it. "You too."

With no more business, Conrad and Darber departed, pedaling back onto the street leading to the state road. The doctor let out a soft breath. "Bandits? Sounds like the Wild West out here."

"I wish I had better news, but even the smallest towns are in a pinch. The farms are crowded with refugees, so they can't regularly supply the stores with food. They got to feed everyone on the land. Hooper City at least got back on its feet with a few new crops. If they can get some of the damned stuff canned, they may have a chance to last through the winter." Conrad scowled. "But you heard the story. They have to guard the food on top of everything else that's going on here."

As Conrad walked his bike back on the road, he noticed Darber's expression. The doctor opened his mouth, and seemed ready to say something. But quickly, he closed his mouth and turned away.

Something's eating this man, Conrad thought. There were too many signs for him to dismiss it. First, though, he wanted to get him home. Some questions just would have to wait.

———

VANDER'S FIST pushed open the glass door all the way, easily allowing Blake and Lance into the motor-cycle shop. At least it used to be a motorcycle shop. Now it served as one of Kurt's main storehouses in addition to a service point for the few vehicles Kurt was able to salvage from the solar event. As it turned out, some of the automobiles around town were old enough to have survived, as they didn't possess elec-tronics that could be fried.

Juan was one of the guys who took care of them.

"Juan!" Blake called. "Hey, Juan!"

A tall, thin man ran up from behind a tool chest. "Hey, Blake! Vander! What's going on?"

"We need guns," Vander said. "Guns and sharp as hell knives. We're going hunting."

Juan smiled. "Ah, the best of the best, right? Now, when you say hunting, you mean animal or person?"

"Doctor Darber's disappeared." Blake's boots crunched on the loose rocks inside the facility. Juan was not a guy who cared much about cleanliness, or anything else beyond his immediate interest. "We think he peeled out of town with some guy named Conrad Drake, or at least that's what this kid here tells us."

"Ah." Juan curled his fingers in an imitation of someone holding a gun. "Homo sapiens. Toughest prey out there, right? We want him back alive, I'm sure."

"Yeah, but we're probably going to spill some blood on this." Blake narrowed his eyes. "So, lethal and non-lethal."

Before Juan could speak again, the glass door to the shop opened once more. Blake turned, ready to show annoyance at the interruption. But then he froze, and his expression morphed into surprise, if not a tinge of horror.

The man wasn't tall. In fact, he only dwarfed Lance in height. Otherwise, Vander, Blake and Juan all surpassed him by at least six inches. Much of his appearance was obscured by his clothing, with even his head seeming to disappear inside a high-collared jacket and a big hat. Other than that, his only visible skin was on his left hand, for a black leather glove sheathed his right hand. His eyes looked dingy yellow, and they barely moved. When Hunter wanted to look at something, he turned his whole head in that direction.

"Hunter," Blake said, sounding almost shocked.

Hunter turned his neck with the smoothness of a robot. "Blake. I see you're already working hard to retrieve the doctor."

"Yeah. In fact, we were arming ourselves now." Blake took a slow step backward, almost as if he hoped Hunter wouldn't notice.

"As expected," Hunter said.

Chills ran across Lance's skin. Hunter was Kurt's right hand man. When he showed up, it was like you were hearing from the mouth of Kurt himself. Nobody in town was more reverential, more subservient to Kurt than Hunter was, to the point that some of the men wondered if the man was possessed. Lance thought the idea was silly, something superstitious people bought into, but as he observed the calm, glided movements of Hunter and the unnerving serenity in the man's eyes, Lance wondered if this man wasn't touched by the devil himself in some way.

Hunter pulled out a set of truck keys. "Here," he

said, "Phoenix has given you the go-ahead to use one of the trucks to bring the doctor back."

Juan reached out and took them. "He must be pissed as hell to give us the keys, no?"

"Phoenix is concerned. If you don't return with his doctor or a suitable explanation, then he will be angry," Hunter replied dryly.

Juan's smile faded a little. "Well, I don't guess it's too late to find someone else to take this job, right?" Neither Blake nor Vander ventured a response.

"Phoenix has complete confidence in your abilities," Hunter said. "So don't prove him wrong."

Hunter then pushed open the door and showed himself out. It wasn't until Hunter was out of sight that Vander finally blurted out, "'Phoenix!' What a crock of shit. I don't mind working for the man, but this god complex shit really drives me up the wall."

Lance scratched his arm. "Phoenix" was Kurt's nickname. Lance didn't know why, as it sounded like Kurt was being named for a major American city, but apparently the word had a different meaning than just Arizona's biggest city. It was some kind of legendary creature, but Lance couldn't recall what it was.

"That 'god complex shit' keeps a lot of locals in line," Blake said. "A lot of folks think God turned his back on them, so they're shopping around for a new god. Kurt just happened to fit the bill."

Vander just sneered. Juan, however, allowed his full smile to return. "Well, I guess I should pack some snacks, too, before we leave."

"Hey." Vander seized Juan by the shoulder. "Get the gear first. And double it. Double it all. I'm not getting Kurt pissed at us for failing this."

Juan grabbed Vander's hand. "Sure." Then he pulled. Vander allowed Juan to pry off his hand. If Vander wanted to, he could have seriously bruised Juan, but the henchman had no time to do anything other than make a point.

Juan then turned to the back room and pushed open the doors. Inside was a small arsenal of guns and knives hanging from the wall.

"So, I guess I can wish you guys good luck," Lance said. "I mean, you got the map and everything."

"You're coming with us," Blake said.

Fresh sweat poured down Lance's face. "But you don't need me."

"If this goes down badly, you're our insurance policy," Vander said as he took a sidearm from Juan.

"Okay! Okay!" Lance exclaimed, waving his hands. "But I'm getting a gun too, right?"

Vander, Blake and Juan all turned and looked at him. Then they burst out laughing.

"I like this guy." Juan waved his finger at Lance. "I'm glad he's coming. He can make us laugh the whole trip."

Lance swallowed. This whole mess was getting worse by the minute. Lance feared by the end of the week, he'd be pushing up daisies.

———

DARBER EYED the homestead as Conrad approached the porch. "Still looks in tip top shape since I last saw her." Then he tilted his head toward the right side of the home. "Well, except for those windows." The nearest window still was covered with a piece of wood.

"There's still damage that we haven't fixed yet. I hope you're not unnerved by a few bullet holes in the walls, but we must set our priorities. Between bringing in crops and tending to the animals, I'd say we'll just have to get used to Swiss cheese walls for a while," Conrad said.

As Darber closed in on Conrad's house, the damage from Derrick Wellinger's siege became more apparent. Every now and then he'd spot a cut or a splice in the house wall near a window. It was clear the windows took the brunt of the damage, as the gunmen were trying to take out whoever was inside, and shooting through the glass was the easiest way to do it.

"Unbelievable," Darber said.

"I wish we would have gotten back under the cover of darkness," Conrad said.

"Why? I thought you told me you took care of Derrick Wellinger and his men," Darber said.

Conrad halted as his boots hit the porch deck. A middle-aged woman with bleached blonde hair and an expression that stared daggers at Conrad stood there in the open doorway.

Conrad licked the insides of his mouth. "That's why."

Darber looked to Conrad, then to Camilla in the door. "Did something go wrong?"

Camilla held up the note that Conrad had written. "Damn, Conrad, not even a goodbye," she said.

Conrad slipped his hands in his pants pockets. "It was kind of a spur of the moment thing."

"Oh yes, nowadays taking off for a night is like going to the grocery store to buy eggs!" Camilla took a few steps toward him. "I mean, come on. You can't just pop in and say, 'Hey, I got to go fetch the doctor, see ya soon'?"

"I didn't want you to worry too much," Conrad said. "Besides, I know you'd want to stick to me like glue."

"You're right about that. Well, you're back and the house isn't full of fresh bullet holes except the one I shot in the wall when I read your letter," Camilla said.

Conrad closed his eyes. "Cammie..."

"Just kidding. Come on in, both of you." Camilla turned and walked inside.

Darber looked at Conrad. "Are you sure you two are okay?"

Conrad stiffened up. "Damn sure."

CHAPTER SIX

OUTSIDE IN THE BACKYARD, in the shadow of the house, Conrad gazed at the row of freshly canned jars before him on the table. "Now that is a thing of beauty," he said. Darber was right there with him, examining the jars of fruits and vegetables.

Sarah smiled. "I was just thinking how many trips to the grocery I'd have saved if I knew how to do this." Then she laughed.

"Think you'll feel the same way when it's time to slaughter some pigs?" Conrad raised an eyebrow.

Sarah coughed. "You probably have me there."

Conrad reached for one of the jars, but Sarah slapped him away. "Don't touch it! It's still cooling!"

Conrad held the hand that Sarah slapped. "Yes, ma'am," he said softly, coating his tone with a touch of sarcasm. Then he glanced at Darber and rattled his head.

Camilla picked up a jar of carrots at the very end,

one that already had cooled off. "I know it's not pretty, but soon enough, when we slaughter some of the animals, we'll have a load of meat that'll take us through winter and into spring. Oh Conrad, you said you went to Hooper City. Did you get a chance to show Nigel our handiwork?"

Conrad nodded. "He was impressed. He definitely could use some of our jars. But he didn't bring good news about Hooper City. It seems there's thieves afoot going after their crops, and some of them are from Derrick's little band."

Camilla lightly slapped her forehead. "God."

"Yeah, he advised us to steer clear of town for a bit until they can get some protection organized," Conrad said, "to keep the cans from being stolen."

Sarah placed her hands on her hips. "I hate to ask this, but do *we* have anything to worry about?"

"That Derrick's boys might come back?" Conrad exhaled loudly. "Could be, though I'd like to think we put the fear of God in them and they got the hint that we're not easy pickings."

"I doubt it," Camilla said. "Bullies always go after the low hanging fruit. They know our bite's pretty deep."

"True, but the danger's always going to be there, whether it's Derrick's boys or somebody else who's desperate for food and resources," Conrad said. "We just have to stay prepared for what the next day will bring. That's all we can do."

Darber braced himself on the jar table with both

hands. "I hate to cut the tour short, Conrad, but I'm exhausted. I'm not as young as I used to be." He chuckled. "Or rather, I'm not in as good a shape as I should be. How about I take some time off my feet? That couch in the front room looks pretty inviting to me."

"Sure." Conrad turned to the house's side door. "In fact, that couch has a roll-out bed. You can plant yourself there for the night. I'd give you a guest room, but as you can imagine, I've got a few too many guests here."

———

DARBER LET OUT a contented sigh as he laid back on the roll-out bed. Conrad and Sarah stood off to the side. "This place reminds me of my uncle's farm in Jefferson. I spent almost every weekend for three years going there to help mow the grass. They didn't have central air, so a lot of the rooms felt like this." He closed his eyes. "Got some happy memories there."

"I did look into solar-powered fans before the solar event hit. I even rigged our shower with solar energy, but I never got a chance to try it with a fan," Conrad said.

Darber opened his right eye. "You have a running shower?"

"Surprised, huh?" Sarah laughed.

"Actually, I was more surprised Conrad didn't have

a mess of hamsters running on a giant wheel to generate power for the whole house," Darber said.

Conrad shook his head. "Sorry, Ron. I'm not that good. Besides, I would have used squirrels."

Sarah flashed Conrad a wry look. "I'm joking," he replied.

"I sure hope so. It's hard to tell sometimes." Sarah's smile grew a little wider. "How about we drag Liam and Carla in here to meet Doctor Darber? They've been out there long enough, especially poor Carla."

Conrad turned to Darber. "I'll return with our youngsters."

"I won't be going anywhere. Actually, I'll try not to dose off." Darber stretched his arms.

Conrad left, but Sarah stuck around. "So, how long have you known Conrad?"

"About six years. I worked out of an office with another doctor named John Waldo, but he retired and left town. He'd see me for various things."

"Like what?" Sarah asked.

"Nothing too serious. Can't get into any detail. Patient confidentiality," Darber answered. "You understand."

Sarah nodded. "Right. No, I was just wondering about Conrad, what's he been up to in the past several years. I don't know much about his life since..." She grasped her right arm. "Since we parted ways."

Darber sat up. "Well, I'm not sure what I could

talk about. Conrad's very much what you see. A bigger thinker than he is a talker."

Sarah folded her arms. "Did he ever talk about me?"

Darber smiled. "Patient confidentiality."

"Oh good grief." Sarah chuckled.

Darber chuckled with her. "Actually, he talked as little as he could about his past. I knew he was divorced. I didn't learn much else about his family, except that he hadn't seen his son in many years." The doctor looked up at the ceiling. "Quite a surprise to see how things have changed for him."

Sarah inhaled a deep breath. "For both of us."

————

"IT'S A BEAUT!" Juan shouted as he walked beside the red four-wheel-drive truck.

The truck was housed inside this small service garage on Kurt's orders. Even though the vehicle was almost four decades old, it had been well maintained and refitted a few times during its lifespan. It was clean and well-serviced, and its set of high tires made it a vehicle that could handle almost any terrain.

"Fully gassed and ready to go, right?" he asked as he turned to Blake, Vander and Lance.

"It may be ready to go, but I'm not." Vander yawned. "It's getting dark out there. I want to catch some sleep before we go hunting."

Juan leaned against the truck's back door. "You sure Kurt doesn't want us to get going ASAP?"

"Where? The doc's probably still wandering around in the dark." Vander shook the road map in his hand. "Give him time to get to where he's going, then we pop in and grab him."

"We still need time to load up some food for the road," Blake said, while casting a glance at the glass doors leading to the section of the maintenance shop.

Lance wondered if he expected Hunter to show up again. This maintenance shop was under close supervision by Kurt's men, even more than Juan's shop down the street. These three guys might be the toughest brutes Lance had met, but even their legs shook at the thought of Kurt's wrath.

"No kidding." Vander pushed past Lance, almost knocking the young man down to the concrete floor. "I'm not going out there with nothing to shove in my stomach. I want to get those goddamn snacks."

Lance thought this might be a chance to get on their good side. "Do you want me to get you the food? I mean, I know Sam bundles it up for the men. I can run down there and grab a, uh, a package."

"Screw off," Vander said. "You're not going anywhere until we get the doc back."

"But it's getting late. I need to get back to the attic to get some sleep," Lance replied.

"You're sleeping here," Blake said as he yanked open the driver's side door of the truck.

Lance looked around. There was nothing here but

the truck, an oil pan, and a few shelves containing oil cans, grease tubes, a couple of car batteries, and spray cans of starter fluid. "On the ground?"

"Unless you can defy gravity and sleep on the ceiling, sure," Juan said, while showing off his teeth in a grin.

Lance cringed. Sleeping on hard concrete. It could be worse, but as he crouched low to the ground and inhaled an old odor of automobile fumes, he wondered how much worse it could be.

Doctor Darber, he thought, with a tinge of anger. *Why'd he have to skip town and throw me into this mess?* He was beginning to hope some bad end would befall the doctor for all the trouble Vander and Blake had rained down on Lance. He gripped his arms tightly. Hadn't he been through enough hell working for Derrick? How could life get any worse than that?

As he sat on the hard ground, another part of him wished he had thought of skipping town when he had had the chance. Given how Kurt's men treated everyone in Davies, who could blame Darber for wanting to get out of here?

Maybe this is my chance, Lance thought. *If I'm out of town, surely I can give these three the slip. It's not like Kurt will send a bunch of guys to hunt me down. Who am I? I'm not a doctor or anybody useful. I'm just a grunt worker.*

Perhaps getting mixed up in this pursuit of Darber wasn't the worst thing to hit Lance Wilkins after all.

———

"It's unfortunate that I don't have an ultrasound available for you," Darber said to Carla, who was seated right beside him on the bed in her and Liam's bedroom. Conrad, Liam and Sarah stood at the doorway, watching. Darber's medical bag lay on the bed, unzipped. Darber had finished putting his tools back inside.

Conrad had brought Liam and Carla in as promised. Darber then took Liam into the bedroom with Carla and shut the door for a private examination of Carla. After a while, Liam emerged to let Conrad and Sarah inside. Tom and Camilla remained busy with their tasks.

Darber smiled gently. "But, I can say that with what I have, examining you was no more difficult than someone who could have examined Liam. And I am happy to say all signs are looking good."

Carla clapped her hands together. "Great!"

"Thank God," Sarah said.

Conrad clasped Liam's shoulder tight. Liam looked at his dad and smiled.

"I don't guess you can tell if I'm having a boy or a girl?" Carla asked.

Darber shook his head. "Sorry. I suppose in this case, life will have to spring a surprise or two."

Carla looked down at her stomach. "So, what do I have to look forward to? Any mood swings or binge eating in my future?" Then she flashed Liam a grin. "Biting my mate's head off like a praying mantis?"

Liam mockingly stepped behind Conrad as if his old man was acting as cover from an attacking Carla.

Darber chuckled. "Well, I can draw up a list of what you might expect as your pregnancy progresses. It's not the same for all ladies. But I would tell you to avoid any dangerous work, including anything that can puncture the skin or cause falls. Also stay away from dangerous chemicals. We're particularly concerned with anything that can harm your fetus."

Carla turned her left foot from side to side. "I hate the idea of not pulling my own weight."

"Well you'll be pulling a lot of weight soon." Liam chuckled softly. "Don't worry. We can handle everything."

"We also should put together a list of supplies for a delivery," Darber said. "You're still early in your pregnancy, so we have time. I'll also give Liam some pointers on helping you breathe during contractions."

"Contractions?" Carla grimaced. "That's right, I forgot having a baby involves a lot of screaming and pain."

"There's a lot of screaming and pain after the baby's born. It doesn't end there," Conrad said.

Sarah slapped him on the chest. "Conrad!"

"As God is my witness, Liam put you through some sleepless nights trying to get him to go to bed," Conrad replied calmly.

Liam shook his head. "I'm glad I don't remember what it was like to be a baby."

"Eating, crying, and pooping until you learned the words 'I want.' Then it was just eating, crying, pooping and saying 'I want' until you were three and a half," Conrad said.

Carla reached out and took Liam's arm. "I guess it's not too late to build us a private log cabin in the fields, huh?" She laughed.

"Naaah. Who would help you two with dinner?" Conrad looked out the window at the setting sun. "Darber and I have had a long trip today. Let's get the table set with a good welcome dinner for our guest."

CHAPTER SEVEN

BLAKE PUT ON THE BRAKES, bringing the truck to a halt. "This is as far as we drive," he said. "Now we walk the rest of the way."

Lance quickly followed Vander out the door, least he get shoved by Juan close behind him. Blake brought up the rear. Once he locked the truck doors, Blake pointed to the road a few steps away. He had driven them up to this point, then pulled off the road. They were willing to use gas to get them out here, but not use more than needed for this job.

Juan grasped the opposite ends of the street map. Lance had marked the path along State Road 22 right to Conrad's ranch. "Looks like we've got a couple of hours' walk," he said, "Since we didn't spot anybody, there's nobody to warn him we're coming."

Vander then slapped Lance on the back. "And when we get there, the little dipshit here will go to the door and call for the doctor."

Lance froze. "Wait, you want me to go to Conrad's door?"

"Hey, the little guy's hearing's working," Juan said with a laugh.

"But I can't!" Lance said as he shook. There was no way he could face Conrad again!

Vander glowered at him. "Funny. No one said you had a choice, little man."

"But-but...he'll recognize me! I was shooting at his house, his family! He'll know it's me, and he'll..." Lance gulped. "He'll blow my ass away."

"This little guy's so scared he'll piss himself," Juan said, chuckling.

Lance backed up a step. "I'm telling you, I can't do it. I can't let him see me!"

Vander grabbed a fistful of Lance's shirt. "Oh, you're going to knock on his door, or I'm going to throw your ass right into it."

Blake stopped short of the road. "Wait." He turned and faced Vander. "Little bug here may have a point. This Conrad guy sees him and freaks out, he'll probably lock down his whole ranch."

Vander released Lance, who wasted no time in scampering away a few steps, but not so far away that none of the men gave chase.

Juan pointed to Vander and Blake. "But he hasn't seen us before, so he doesn't know shit about what we're going to do."

"I don't know." Vander frowned, pointing his thumb back at Lance. "He makes this Conrad fella sound like a cracked-up gun totting nutjob. I'm not going to risk my ass."

"It's Kurt's doctor," Blake replied. "You want to go back to Kurt empty-handed?"

Vander twitched. He didn't have to verbally respond to communicate that he sure as hell didn't.

"Fine. We go there ourselves. But what do we do about him?" Juan pointed to Lance.

Lance smiled. "I'll just...guard the truck." He backed up toward the vehicle. "Yeah. I can do that. Make sure no one steals it."

Vander suddenly smiled. "Hear that?" He turned to Blake and Juan. "He's volunteering to guard the truck." Blake and Juan then narrowed their eyes and nodded.

———

LANCE WAS SLAMMED hard into the truck's back seat. Ropes bound his arms behind his back, with a second pair binding his legs. Vander, smiling at his handiwork, grasped the back door, ready to slam it shut.

"Hey!" Lance cried out, "What are you doing? I-I'm not going to run away!"

Blake smiled. "You don't think we're that stupid, do you? Be glad we didn't throw you in the trunk. That's only because we don't know if you'd get enough air to live until we get back."

"But what I have to go pee?" Lance cried.

Juan shrugged. "Who's stopping you?"

Vander leaned inside a little. "You're always bitching that you got too much work to do. So, now you can rest in the truck. Wait for us to get back with the doctor. Oh, and if we don't find him..." Vander drew a knife from his belt. "You'll get to rest alright, in peace."

Lance's eyes widened. Juan laughed heartily as Vander shut the door. Then Blake seized the keys from his pocket and locked the door before the trio embarked on their journey.

Lance struggled. No, it was no good. These ropes were too tight. He couldn't move his hands. All he could do was roll around on the seat. His only hope was that they could find Doctor Darber and bring him back here.

———

CONRAD MASSAGED his left foot through his sock again. The pain finally was subsiding. His left boot lay on the floor beside him. In another few minutes, he'd be out of the dining room seat and back outside tending to the water well.

Just then, Sarah emerged into the room, freshly dressed, but still yawning, her eyes tired. When she spotted Conrad, she stopped and leaned against the wall. "Well, here's a surprise. Thought I'd get another goodbye note. Instead I get the real deal sitting at the table."

"I was planning on another trip, but I found out I

had a date with a large brick." Conrad massaged his foot again. "She had other plans."

Sarah shook her head. "Is it bad?"

"Not really. Just a case of me being stupid enough to not look where I was going. Damn. I really am getting a little slower in my older age." Then he narrowed his eyes at Sarah. "Now you heard me say 'older,' not 'old.' Crucial difference there."

Sarah felt a lock of her graying hair. "I'm in the same boat," she said as she approached. "Would you be okay if I sat down?"

"Go ahead," Conrad said.

Sarah took a seat. As she sat down, it occurred to Conrad that this was the closest they had been to each other in a long time. In fact, they had not been alone in the same room together, not even since the rescue from Redmond.

"I hope I didn't piss you off too much by taking off for Darber. I guess I'm just too used to doing things in the moment," Conrad said.

"You brought me a doctor that's going to help deliver my grandbaby. I can't be too mad about that." Sarah smiled, but it was a sad smile.

Conrad could tell she wasn't happy about something. "Maybe I'm done being too mad about a lot of things, especially when it comes to you." She sat back. "In fact, I've misjudged you, way, way too much. You've been far kinder to me than I deserve. I don't even I thanked you for putting me and Tom up."

"You did," Conrad said, "Trust me, I heard the words."

Sarah sighed. "I think that was a polite 'thank you.' I don't know how much I meant it."

Conrad cleared his throat quietly. Sooner or later, a moment like this was coming. The past wanted to rear its head, inflamed by the recent gathering at his father's grave. A question burned in his mind, and he wasn't sure if he was wise to ask it. Still, he felt he wouldn't have peace unless he heard Sarah address it.

"Sarah?" Conrad asked, "Do you think I was the man who couldn't stay in the valley?"

Sarah smiled hard, trying to hold back laughter. "Conrad, you're going to have to speak a little more plainly for me. I'm afraid I'm still not in your world."

"I understand. You remember the movie *Shane*?"

"Yeah," Sarah leaned a little closer. "It's been ages since I saw it. Actually, the last time I saw it was with you."

"Well, in the movie, Shane's the guy who gets rid of the gunfighters in the valley and brings peace back to the land. But at the end of the movie, he rides off. He wanted to rid the valley of all the guns, but it turned out he was one of them. He's the last gun, who can't stay. He can't stay and enjoy the peace he created because he's a man of violence. I'm just wondering if at the end of the day, I bring too much of that fury under a roof, if I'm the guy who can't stay in the valley when all the outlaws have been dealt with."

Sarah just stared at him. Finally, she said, slowly, "Conrad, it was just a movie."

Conrad tilted his head in surprise.

"It's not real. It's just a story." Sarah laughed once. "If anyone's wondering if they belong under a roof, it's me. This is your house, and everything here plays by your rules. I'm the oddball here. I'm the one who doesn't fit! The world not too long ago announced that you, Conrad Drake, were right about everything. So, you don't have anything to worry about." She sat back. "No, I don't think you're the man who couldn't stay in the valley. But, once upon a time, I thought you weren't. And I and Liam had to live with that choice for almost thirty years."

"But perhaps it was meant to be." Conrad pointed to the ceiling. "It all brought us to this place, a home in the midst of the worst catastrophe mankind has seen in ages."

"Maybe. But what did I give up? Could Liam have had a brother, a sister, siblings, a life with you? Could his life have been richer? Hell, maybe he could have gotten to know your wild and nutty family a little better."

"We're just going off the rails thinking that," Conrad said. "We can't change the past, and we can't give Liam anything back that he's lost because we split. He's about to become a dad himself. And if I let any bitter feelings get in the way of what he's got to be, if it got in the way of what we have now, then I didn't deserve to be your husband in the first place."

Sarah nodded. "I feel the same way."

"Then I guess we can say certain things are over and done with," Conrad said.

Sarah smiled again. "Tell me about Liam. How did it feel when you first saw him after all the time apart?"

Conrad rested his head back. "Oh God, what a time that was. I didn't think I'd ever see him again, and then there he was at my front door with Carla beside him. They looked like us at that age, remember? We were an unstoppable force. We felt like we could take on the whole world. They came to me with this crazy idea of braving a town run by lunatics and gangsters to save you. And I'll be damned, but by the end we pulled it off, even if he and Carla had to sit the last part out."

Sarah rested her head in her hands, which were propped up by her elbows on the table. Her expression seemed dreamy, with her eyes staring out into the air past Conrad. She had to be as proud of her son as Conrad was.

Conrad stretched out his left leg. "Funny thing, he takes after you a lot. I guess some of me is in there too, but not in his mouth. He lets you know what he thinks, a lot more than I can."

"And it was all good between you? No fights, no angry words?" Sarah asked.

"Not a one. God knows I don't want any of that between us. But that doesn't mean I can't lay down the law. I know I'm his father, but around here I'm like the king of a small country. With our world gone to pieces, we can't rely on the government or any ruling authority but ourselves. So, I guess I got to be whatever I need to be to keep this household going into the future."

Sarah released her hands, then lifted her head. "I think I know what you mean."

Conrad thought of Sarah decked out with those guns the other night, ready for her patrol around the ranch. He was sure she understood what he meant. Clearly, she had decided to take on whatever role she needed to take on to handle this new reality.

"Say, would you like a cup of coffee?" Conrad asked.

Sarah chuckled. "Conrad, you hurt your foot. I'm not making you get up for me."

"Oh, come on, it's no big deal." Conrad got up and swiftly ignored the tinge of pain that shot up his left foot. Then he marched through the nearby door to the kitchen and fixed some coffee.

A few minutes later, he returned to the table with two mugs. He passed one to Sarah. "Thank you," she said.

Conrad took a sip from his. Sarah set her mug down. "You're still hurting."

"Am not," he replied.

"Liar."

Conrad rolled his eyes. "Let's say it's a soft ache and we'll call it even."

"You really haven't changed." Sarah then took another drink. "And I'm glad you haven't."

A few sips later, Conrad set his mug down and looked at Sarah. "Whatever you might think about what happened between us." He wiggled his right index finger back and forth between her and him. "Even if it hurt at the time, the end result was this place." Then he pointed to the ceiling above, then to the walls and doorways leading to the kitchen, the hallway, and the living room. "If this was our destined place, perhaps there's nothing more to say about what's past."

Sarah drank again from her mug, then said a quiet, "Right."

CHAPTER EIGHT

Blake tapped the chain link fence that ran parallel to the road. A ranch lay on the other side. The soft sounds of goats bleating had lured Blake, Juan and Vander in this direction. Vander, with his hand shielding his eyes from the sun, pointed out the homestead off in the distance.

"This is it," Blake said, "We've hit the spot on the map where the kid drew the line."

The party hiked along the fence. Thanks to the overgrowth of vines and weeds on the fence and near it, their presence wouldn't go easily detected. Still, Blake told them to watch out for anybody on guard. They'd likely be holding a rifle or other firearm.

As they closed the gap between themselves and the homestead, they spotted one of the ranch's hands —a thin Caucasian man in an oversized shirt hauling a bucket of picked vegetables. He approached the fence line.

Blake turned to Vander. "Don't say anything. I'll take it from here." Blake then straightened his jacket collar. "Remember, act neighborly."

Soon Tom walked close enough to the fence that he could spot Blake, Juan and Vander. At the same time, Blake raised his hand. "Hello!" he shouted, "Afternoon to you."

Tom stopped in place. "Uh, good afternoon," he said.

"Crop season, right?" Blake asked with a laugh, "Looks like you got a pretty sweet haul."

"Sweet," Juan repeated.

Tom put down his bucket. "You could say that. So, how I can help you?"

"Oh, it's nothing. We're looking for a friend of ours. He's a doctor. Ronald Darber. Seems he went missing and we're worried about him."

"Really?" Tom asked.

"Yep. A little birdie said he came out this way," Blake said. "You're the only ranch we see for miles. Maybe he showed up here for a night or two. Is he here?"

Tom swallowed. "Well, I'm not sure," he said uneasily. "I'm just...one of the hands. They don't tell me everything. But I could go ask."

"You do that." Blake smiled, showing off his teeth. "Hey, we'll just head up to your door and wait for your answer."

Tom nodded. "Right." Then he picked up the bucket and walked, very quickly, toward the home.

———

Darber handed Liam the cluster of small yellow pages. "First pack of breathing exercises, complete with diagrams."

Liam took them and flipped through the pages. "You write great for a doctor," he said.

"That's because I used pictures." Darber chuckled. "Wasn't going to take any chances."

"But you are going to show me this?" Liam asked as he studied Darber's notes.

"Sure. Conrad just wanted me to get everything down on paper. I can understand. You might not know when, well, if, any of us aren't available for some reason," Darber said.

Liam turned to his dad, who stood in the doorway between the living room and the hall. "Sage stuff, isn't it?" Conrad asked. Then he smiled. "I always knew Ron was a good artist. It's good for him to get this stuff down with pictures."

The scene was interrupted when Tom approached through the hallway, his shirt slicked with sweat and vegetation hanging off his body. "We have...guests..." he panted.

"Guests?" Conrad asked, his expression suddenly turning to a frown.

"Three guys at the fence. They were asking about Doctor Darber," Tom answered quickly.

Darber's cheeriness instantly melted away into

shock and horror. "Three men?" he asked, sounding if someone had punched him in the gut.

"What's the deal?" Conrad turned to Darber. "Why would anybody be looking for you?" Then he craned his head in Tom's direction. "Did they say they were from Davies?"

"Didn't say, but I tell you I didn't trust those guys. One of them looks like he's made of solid rock, his fist could flatten your skull with one hit. They were all wearing jackets. They could be armed. I couldn't see."

"What else?" Darber asked, "Appearance, like beards or skin color? What did you see?"

"The big guy had red hair and a matching beard. There was a thin guy, brown skin, probably Hispanic. The guy who talked to me was shorter, had this strange drawl in his voice."

"That could be Blake," Darber whispered.

Conrad took a step closer to Darber. "You know these folks, don't you?"

Darber shook his head. "I'm so sorry. I never thought they would find me here."

The doctor turned to his suitcase on the couch. "I must go. They'll come here and they won't stop unless I go back with them."

Tom looked out the window. "Well, they're out there now in front of the door."

Camilla turned to the hall. "Damn. I'll get some arms and move their asses off our property."

"Wait!" Darber raised his hands. "You can't go

against Kurt's men! More will come here if I don't go back with them!"

"Kurt?" Conrad made a fist. "Who the hell is Kurt? Dammit, I knew you were fidgeting like a scared rabbit back on the road. You wanted out of Davies bad. It's because of these fellas, isn't it?"

"Yes! Yes! I should have told you, but I thought I could escape, disappear, leave it all behind!" Darber shook his head.

"Look, you can dither all you want." Camilla marched into the hall. "I'm getting the heavy artillery."

Darber braced his head with his hands. "No! This will turn out bad. I've got to—I've got to talk to them." He cringed. "I can't. No, I've got to!"

Then he turned and ran for the front door. He unlocked it, then flung it open and rushed outside, shutting it behind him.

"Ron!" Conrad called, narrowly missing him. "Dammit, come back here!"

———

THERE WAS no turning back now. Ronald Darber was confronting one of his worst nightmares short of Kurt himself. He had met Blake, Juan and Vander off and on during the past month, but never ran into the three men together. Basically, he was doomed. He was no fighter. Physically, he was no match for even a man half the size of Vander, Blake or Juan. His only hope was to talk his way out of this.

"Well, look who it is," Blake said, almost stone-faced. "You didn't even leave a goodbye note. Kind of rude, isn't it?"

"There was a medical emergency to take care of," Darber said gruffly. "You know how in demand doctors are nowadays."

"All the way out here? That's one hell of a house call, Doc," Juan said. "The phones don't work. No one can text you. So, what's the deal? Seems like you just up and left."

"No! It's true. I was just repaying a favor for a friend, that's all," Darber said.

"And how long was that favor gonna last?" Vander asked.

"Kurt, the Phoenix, he's the only friend you got." Blake advanced one step toward Darber. "You're his, pal. He says go, you go. He says stay, you stay. He didn't tell you to go, Doc. That means you're in deep, deep shit."

"And so's anybody who helped you out." Vander looked over Darber's shoulder to the house door behind him.

Darber quaked. "What? No, no. I'll go back with you. Just don't hurt Conrad!"

"Conrad?" Blake cocked his head. "So, that crazy old rancher does live here. He's the guy who brought you here, right?"

"No!" Darber shouted.

"Stop lying, you sack of shit!" Blake then shoved Darber to the porch floor.

"We got word that a guy named Conrad Drake lives here, and he's a little messed up in the head, got big guns and all that stuff. Kurt's going to want a little compensation for this trouble. Maybe this Conrad's got some guns? Some sweet crops? Animals?" Vander then grabbed Darber and held him up as Blake cracked his knuckles. "Let's talk."

————

THE SOUND of Camilla's boots turned Conrad's head from the front door. She hastily had donned an over-the-shoulder belt along with a waist belt, both containing firearm magazines. She also clutched a pair of rifles. Stopping, she handed one to Conrad.

"What's the deal?" she asked quietly.

"A lot of fussing going on. Don't know how long that's going to last. I checked, but I didn't see any guns in their hands. But it's hard to tell through that damned peephole."

Suddenly, one of their visitors raised his voice even louder. "Stop lying, you sack of shit! We got word that a guy named Conrad Drake lives here, and he's a little messed up in the head, got big guns and all that stuff. Kurt's going to want a little compensation for this trouble. Maybe this Conrad's got some guns? Some sweet crops? Animals? Let's talk."

"Damn," Conrad said in low voice. "We got to get

him inside. These bastards sound like they mean business. Camilla, go around the side, catch them from behind. I'll open the door and drag him back in."

Then he turned to Camilla, but noticed his living room was a little emptier. Camilla, Tom, Sarah and Carla were there. No Liam.

"Where the hell did Liam go?" Conrad asked.

———

LIAM CREPT along the side of the house. The corner of the house was in sight. Now Liam got on his knees. The porch was approaching. He couldn't let their three "visitors" see him until he was right on top of them.

Sweat poured down his face. He was angry. Angry that once again trouble had come to his home. Angry that malevolent men were at his door. No, he would not let things spin out of control as they did when Derrick Wellinger laid siege to his dad's homestead. Now Liam was going to take the fight to the bad guys for a change.

I can't just go in guns blazing, Liam thought. *Doctor Darber could get hit by accident. I have to do this just right.*

He pulled out his taser. Then he crawled below the porch's floor level, only raising his head enough to peer through the banister posts.

A big guy was holding Darber up as a smaller man barked at the doctor. "So, what does Conrad have in there? How many people? More men? Or is it just some ladies and a kiddie or two?"

"Look, you tell me what you want, and I'll have Conrad bring it out. There's no need for guns or killing!" Darber pleaded.

"No, you tell me what he has, and I'll tell you if it's worth taking. I saw a big set of crops out there. This guy looks like he's got a prime farm. I think Kurt would be very interested in this place. Maybe he'll show up and take it for himself."

"No!" Darber cried out.

At that moment, Liam sprang up and shot his taser at the big guy holding Darber. The brute screamed and then released Darber, who landed on the porch with a loud thud.

———

On the other side of the door, Conrad and everyone else heard Darber land with a thud.

Conrad could take no more. He yanked open the front door. The doctor lay on the porch, wincing and clutching his side. Nearby, Vander was on his back, writhing as the taser points immobilized him.

"What the hell?" Blake whipped out his firearm and aimed it at Liam. But Conrad's entry had pulled Blake's attention away from Liam, who leaped over the porch banister and charged him. Blake only had time to turn around before Liam's fist connected with

Blake's face. Both Blake and his firearm fell to the deck.

"Get him inside!" Conrad seized Darber by the shoulders, while Camilla grabbed Darber by his waist. The two adults hauled Darber in quickly, with Sarah shutting the door behind them.

"Wait!" Sarah suddenly looked through the peephole. "God, Liam's out there!"

Conrad got up, just as he heard another thump on the porch. He looked through the peephole. Liam had just cold-cocked Juan on the back of his head. Now all three of the men were down on the porch. Liam quickly was pulling the gun belts off from Darber's assailants.

"Good boy," Conrad whispered. Then he said, louder, "Sarah, Camilla, give Liam backup. And get that trash off my front porch while you're at it." Conrad then turned to Darber, who was lying on the floor, coughing. "I'll make sure they don't land another finger on Ron."

———

LIAM STAGGERED around the side of the house, stumbling back the way he had come. Two gun belts hung over his shoulder, each carrying a gun holster, a knife, and a couple of magazines each. He winced. He had successfully taken the gun belts off two of the men, but that last guy he fought had hit him before Liam could take him out. Unfortunately, it was also the place where he had been shot in the homestead siege.

Lucky shot, he thought. He was in too much pain to hang around there. He had to get these weapons away from the doctor's attackers.

"Liam!" Sarah rushed over to him. "Are you alright?"

"Mom!" Liam let out a gasp. "I'm not bad. One of them just hit me in the spot where I got shot." Then he stopped and let Sarah take the belts off him. "That big guy might still have a gun on him."

"Let Camilla worry about him. I came to get you inside. We got Doctor Darber in." Sarah took Liam by the arm. "C'mon Camilla's waiting on the other side of the gate."

CHAPTER NINE

"BLAKE!" Vander, tired of Blake's unresponsiveness, slapped him across the face. "Dammit, get up already!"

Blake's hand shot up to his face and clenched the cheek where Vander had slapped it. "Shit! What are you doing?"

Vander seized Blake by his shirt and hoisted him up. "They knocked out you and Juan. One of the bastards tased me. They got the doctor inside! We gotta break down the door and get him!"

Blake blinked his eyes. "Damn. Get me...get me up!"

Vander dragged Blake all the way to his feet. Along the way, Blake patted his sides. "My knives. My guns. Where the hell are they?"

"They must have frisked us." Juan braced himself on the banister of the porch. "When me and Blake were knocked out."

Vander looked down at his belt. His knife was gone, lost when he got tasered. But he wasn't fully disarmed as he still had his handgun. "I'm not done yet," he said with a hiss.

Juan started protesting. "They'll be ready for you!"

But Vander pushed Blake aside and stormed off the porch. "Go around back! Get them from behind!"

"Damn it, Vander, you don't know what they got in there!" Blake said as he started chasing after him.

"I want them dead. I want them dead!" he shouted as he stomped through the grass along the side of the house.

"Vander, you idiot! The back is fenced off! You can't get in there!" Juan shouted.

Indeed, the way to the back of the ranch was barricaded by a strong wooden fence and a gate that looked locked and sturdy.

Vander raised his weapon and fired two shots at the gate handle. Both shots struck it and ricocheted off, and while they severely dented the handle, they weren't enough to blow it open.

"The gate's probably reinforced," Blake said, "Face it, we're outmatched."

Before Vander could respond, either with another shot to the gate or a swear word, the grass in front of them suddenly popped. A gunshot from somewhere up ahead had hit the ground, followed by a loud female voice screaming, "Drop it, dickhead!"

Vander's eyes widened. The angry brute suddenly looked scared. "What the hell?"

"What's the matter? You got shit where your brain's supposed to be?" asked the woman, "I said drop it now!"

Vander quickly discarded the gun on the grass. Behind him, Blake and Juan looked around, but there was a large tree growing near the fence that made it hard to see back beyond the gate. With all that cover, it wouldn't be hard for someone to shoot at them.

"Now, you three squirrels turn and run, and I mean quick! If you don't, I'll play target practice with your asses. Now go!" shouted their mystery sniper.

Vander let out a loud profanity before turning and running. Blake and Juan joined him. The three reached the front yard of the homestead, where another gunshot rang out and hit the ground behind them.

Any thought of slowing down was driven immediately from their heads. They fled down the small road that led to State Road 22, then turned and kept on running, never bothering to look back.

———

DARBER STOOD on the small walkway from the porch as Liam and Conrad inspected the front yard and the sides of the house. Sarah stood with Darber, clutching her shotgun. As for the doctor, he just stood there, his face ashen. He just waited as the two men finished their tasks.

"No more weapons back there," Liam said as he emerged from the left side of the house.

"And no more stragglers. Looks like it was just three of them after all," Conrad said as he rejoined Liam by Sarah and Darber.

At that moment, Camilla rode back onto the driveway on the bicycle. "No more signs of them for a couple of miles." She parked the bike, then marched over to Conrad, Liam, Sarah and Darber. "And no more reinforcements, not that I can see."

Conrad turned to Darber. "Do these fellas usually have backup following?"

Darber, still in shock, didn't respond.

"Ron!" Conrad barked with intensity that made even Camilla jump. "Talk to me! Are we going to have more dinner guests?"

Darber shook his head. "I-I don't know. I think that's all that came. They'll have to go back to Kurt and report in."

"Kurt? He's the man running this operation?" Conrad asked.

"Yeah. Yeah, that's right," Darber replied.

Conrad took quick count of all the weapons they had grabbed from Darber's attackers. The men were packing three handguns with five loaded magazines. Each of the men also had packed a sharp knife, with a blade that glistened almost like new. One of them had packed an extendable baton.

"This is enough to kill a man many times over."

Conrad turned slowly to Darber. "Who's this Kurt? Who in God's name did you run afoul of?"

Darber shut his eyes tightly. "I'm sorry. I should have told you sooner."

"Apologize later, after you've told me. Then I'll decide whether to kick your ass or not." Conrad then glanced at Liam. "Pack this stuff and get it inside. Camilla, get the doctor here some tea. I get the feeling we're in for a hell of a story."

————

DARBER WAS SEATED in an easy chair, with Conrad, Tom, Liam, Carla, Sarah and Camilla all standing or seated someplace in front of him or close by. The doctor fidgeted at being the center of such attention, but he finally sighed and got started with his tale.

"This whole mess started out shortly after the solar storm hit. When it became clear the authorities weren't coming to save us, people ran wild. They ransacked stores. Some even went on a rampage through the homes in the affluent areas. There was food there, or so they believed. Homes were torched. One of them belonged to the Walsh family. They were patients of mine. Mrs. Walsh and her son Joshua both were inside the home when the fires began. They had no way to escape. Kurt Marsh, the husband, the father, he was caught in the conflagration. Judging from the news, we thought everyone in that block was incinerated."

Darber took another sip. "But then one day Kurt came to my door. He barely looked human. The flames had scorched his face. He asked for help. Of course, I would do anything I could for him. I couldn't imagine the pain he felt. He was a man with nothing, no home, no property, no family." Darber sighed.

"But I'm not a plastic surgeon. I don't know if even the best surgeon could have restored him, but I did what I could. I made sure he was in no danger physically. He thanked me. He said he understood, and what I had done was enough. He wanted me to be his doctor. I said, fine. I didn't understand what that meant until later."

"I get the feeling Kurt got a lot more possessive for being a grateful patient," Conrad said. "Your town looked a little locked up. And I'm guessing he's the guy who owned that truck I saw run through town."

Darber nodded. "Kurt changed. He would call himself 'Kurt the Phoenix.' The Phoenix is a mythical bird that would die in flames, only to rise again, resurrected from the ashes. Kurt cast himself as something like a legendary figure, to inspire fear. There are more than enough desperate people who will listen to such a man. Before I knew it, he had gathered enough men to impose his will on my town."

Sarah scowled. "Another psychopath with a god complex."

Conrad narrowed his eyes. "We may have to get used to stories like this, Sarah. This is what happens when there's no governing authority to stop such folks."

"Kurt is one of the worst," Darber said. "He won't forgive me for running out on him. He'll want revenge. The thrashing you gave his men will just add more fuel to the fire. If we're lucky, he'll only set his sights on me. But with his men hurt and spurned off your land, I think the Phoenix will want more. He calls his wrath the 'Touch of Hellfire.'"

Nobody said anything. Darber sank his head over his knees.

"I'm sorry. I'll leave at once. I'm sure I'll draw away Kurt's men. I'll take all the blame for it. I'll explain I put you up to it. I bribed you, threatened you, anything to make it clear you're not at fault."

Conrad took a step closer, allowing his shadow to fall over the doctor. "Ron, after what you just told us, there's not a chance this guy is going to overlook us. And in any case, you leaving would just be throwing yourself to the wolves."

"So what? You have your family, a grandchild coming. You have everything in the world to protect." Darber ran a hand over his scalp. "Besides, I led the trouble here. This is my fault. You owe me nothing. I don't blame you if you're furious at me."

"Now that's enough," Conrad said, "Sure, you left out some details. I would have appreciated the full story right off the bat, but that doesn't mean I wouldn't have accepted you into my home. In any case, what's done is done. I need you for the sake of my family."

Darber raised his head. "Are you sure?"

"I won't force you either way," Conrad said. "It's your choice."

"But what if they come?" Darber asked.

Camilla pulled out her shotgun. "They'll regret it within five seconds. Maybe four."

Darber shook. "Conrad..."

"Look, you want the bottom line, Ron? In your hometown you were a prisoner. You may have been alive, but you still were nothing more than Kurt's lapdog, and in my book that's not much of a life. Sure, there's going to be a ton of risk staying here and standing up to Mister Phoenix Arizona or whatever he calls himself..."

Camilla laughed. "'Mister Phoenix Arizona?'"

"Hush, sweetie. Inspirational speech here," Conrad said in deadpan tone. "The point is that we can protect you. I would say we can stop Kurt if he's stupid enough to come making trouble. And once he's gone, you won't have to worry about what he thinks of you ever again. You'll be a free man. I think that's worth fighting for, even dying for. So, what's the verdict?"

CHAPTER TEN

LANCE STIRRED FROM SLEEP A SWEATY, stinking mess. His arms ached. He had worn himself out from weeping, bemoaning his fate. And Juan was right, not having access to a restroom, or a hole in the ground, had not stopped him from using the bathroom. By this point, Lance begged whatever God was out there just to put him out of his misery.

When the truck door suddenly opened, Lance thought he might get his wish.

"Vander!" Blake shouted, "Don't kill him!"

Oh please, Lance thought, *kill me now*.

A massive hand dragged the still-bound Lance out of the truck and slammed him against it. Lance ached so much already that he barely felt it.

Vander was clutching him hard, with Blake grasping Vander's left arm. "We need him alive to tell us everything he knows about this guy."

"He was supposed to tell us everything. He held

back. He didn't say there was another guy with a freaking taser!" Vander roared.

Vander raised Lance high. To add further indignity to the situation, Lance's pants fell down.

Blake glowered at Lance. "You better come real clean, kid, because Vander's hungry for blood, and it's probably going to be yours. How many people does Conrad have on that ranch of his?"

"I don't know," Lance said, whinny, pathetically. "There were two, three people shooting from the house. Then he showed up. There's maybe four. I told you that already."

"Alright." Blake clearly was suppressing his own rage. "You said you and a bunch of guys under Derrick Wellinger tried to kill Conrad and take the land. So, where are the other survivors? Maybe one of them knows more than you do."

Lance panted. "Um...let me think...uh, yeah, Cal! Cal and me, we got out of there, and Cal went to Wellinger's ranch, to take it over. He might still be there. It's not far. We can drive. I'll show you."

"Sounds like a plan." Blake tapped Vander's arm. "Drop him. He's useful again."

Vander snarled at Lance one last time before placing him back on the grass. As Blake unlocked the driver's side door, Juan pointed at Lance's waist and chuckled.

"Man, you peed yourself," he said with a low laugh.

Lance looked down at his exposed boxers. By now,

with all the humiliation and hell he had suffered, he wasn't sure whether to be glad he was alive or not. But at least he talked himself into living another day.

———

DARBER SAT on the roll-out bed. He cast quick glances at the bag lying nearby, then at the front door. His fingers clawed deeply into the folds of the bed fabric. He knew the choice in front of him, yet he couldn't pull the trigger.

He thought of how different he and Conrad were. He was staying under the roof of a man who prepared for the worst, a decisive man who pulled together resources and cunning to create this livable pocket in a world gone sour. And what of Ron Darber? This whole disaster had left him a jittery mess. If he had not possessed valuable skills that others could use and provide him food and water in return, he would have died weeks ago. He had no survival knowledge to speak of beyond what the modern life afforded him. His skills as a doctor helped, but not that much.

Damn it, he thought. *I should have fled town the moment the catastrophe hit. I wouldn't have been drawn into Kurt's web. And I wouldn't have drawn his men to Conrad's home.*

Earlier, Darber had agreed to stay. But he had done so timidly, spoken only quickly enough to end the conversation and move on to the day's other tasks. In truth, he still was not sure.

As he faced the front door, he was less sure now than ever.

Footsteps broke his concentration. Expecting Conrad, he jumped to his feet, but instead Sarah Sandoval rounded the corner. Letting out a soft breath, Darber sat back down.

"Getting close to midnight," Sarah said. "You're still not tired?"

"I could ask the same of you." Darber looked closely at the holster on her belt, then at the shotgun in her hands. "I didn't know Conrad enlisted you as his hired muscle."

"I volunteered," Sarah said curtly. Then she approached him, her boots making thuds on the floor. "When you can't dial 9-1-1 any longer, you pretty much have to be your own policeman, fireman and soldier."

"From what I heard of you, I didn't imagine you'd be the type to take up a gun," Darber said. "I guess you adapted pretty well to the new world."

"I adapted." Sarah bit her lip. "Not well, but I adapted."

"I wasn't given any details, but I was told you were imprisoned for a period. I'm guessing you haven't had contact with a doctor since then. If you require any help, any examination..."

"Doctor, I've been examined more than enough," Sarah said.

"I'm bound by confidentiality," Darber added. "Again, if you need..."

Sarah grasped her gun tighter. "I need nothing. Don't worry. I was given enough food and water and nobody..." Her jaw tightened. "Nobody did anything else to me."

Darber got the message. Drop the subject and move on. "I'm glad to hear that."

Sarah's eyes then focused on Darber's closed bag. "Speaking of adapting, how are you holding up?"

"About half as well as I'd like," Darber replied.

"I can understand. It sounds like you had a rough time with Kurt back home. Guess we both were prisoners of a kind, right?" Sarah's hand grazed the edge of the bed. "So, what are you thinking about now?"

Darber sighed. "My own inadequacies, I suppose. Your former husband sure knows how to make an impression. He has promised to protect me, but part of me wonders if that will be enough."

"So, you're thinking of bailing out?" Sarah said. "Getting the hell out of Dodge? Going off on your own?"

A tremor ran through Darber's arms. "What makes you say that?"

"I've been looking at you from the hall door. You kept staring back and forth from the door to your bag. I remember a few nights when I was trapped in Maggiano's. I'd look at the wooden door to my room and think about busting it down. Maybe I could run away, but then I remembered the whole bloc of rooms was sealed off by metal doors. I guess I can tell when someone else wants to flee somewhere."

Darber nodded. "I suppose you have me dead to rights," he said. "I can't go back to Davies. There are a number of small towns close by, or perhaps a farm. Surely, I'd run into a place where nobody recognizes me, hiding out under a different name. Well, I suppose it's better than leading them here."

"But they'll still show up sooner or later, won't they?" Sarah crossed her arms. "I don't think you can un-crack the eggs here. I think Conrad knew that, too."

"Yes. Yes, I suppose so," Darber said. "I thought leaving would count as doing something. I'm no soldier, no gunfighter, but I thought maybe at least luring them away would make up for leading Kurt's men here. But I can't do anything."

"Nothing except do what Conrad wants you to do, and if it means my grandchild will be born safe and healthy, I think that's good enough." Sarah looked down at her gun. "And if I have to stand guard at the door while you're helping Carla push, then so be it."

Darber raised his head slightly. "Then I'll do what I have to, for your family." Then he stood up. "If you don't mind, I'd like that refresher in gun usage that Conrad promised."

Sarah smiled a little. "Tomorrow. You need sleep, and I need to finish up my patrol for the night."

Darber nodded. "Right. As the Drake home's resident physician, I should understand when the human body requires rest."

Then he sat back on his bed. "Thank you."

"You're welcome. And thanks for coming here. It means the world to us, to me," Sarah replied.

————

SARAH YAWNED DEEPLY before tilting her head up to look at herself in the mirror. *Just one more patrol*, she thought. She had eaten up a lot of time taking watch. At this rate, she'd sleep all the way past noon tomorrow.

A familiar face glided into view behind her. "Hey," Tom said, "Finally ready to get some sleep?"

"God help me, I need it." Sarah ran two hands across her face. She had taken off all her gear, plus her boots and socks, leaving her in a shirt and a pair of khakis. At least changing into bedclothes wouldn't be hard now.

"I thought I overheard you talking to the doctor," Tom said, "Was there something wrong?"

"No." Sarah shook her head. "No, things were fine."

"No medical problems? I should have asked earlier. I guess life's been a blur since we got away from Redmond."

Sarah sighed. "No, nothing like that." She scratched her neck.

Talking to Darber, conversing about adapting to this new world, had made her think a lot about herself. It was true her captivity had left no physical scars, but that didn't mean some emotional damage wasn't inflicted. Tom letting Marco take her was one thing, but she pretty much had put that aside. No, she had something else to tell Tom.

As Tom sat on the bed, letting out a tired yawn, Sarah turned to him. "Actually, Doctor Darber has helped me work out some things." She crossed her arms. "It's been hard to get some things behind me. When I was trapped in Maggiano's warehouse, Maggiano and Jack took very good looks over all the girls there, including me."

Tom sat up. "What do you mean? Sarah, what did they do?"

Sarah shook her head gently. "Don't worry, I told you they didn't have their way with me. But there were days when they'd take everything off." Sarah bristled. "Maggiano liked to be sure his women were in good shape. And if I understood him right, he sure thought I was."

Tom narrowed his eyes. "I wish I had run into him so I could have blown his brains out."

"Well, you did nail Marco." Sarah smiled a bit. "But anyway, it's been hard for me to be comfortable in my skin after that. I close my eyes, and I just feel like I'm being looked over. It's like I'm naked in front of the world."

"Damn," Tom said, "I'm sorry."

"But..." Sarah stepped back. "I can't let that get in the way of us."

Tom held up a hand. "Sarah, I'm not asking a

thing from you. I said that when we came here. You need time."

"Time." Sarah peeled off her shirt, uncovering her black bra. "Tom, most of my life is probably over. We're living in a world where we can get blown away by robbers, bandits, God knows what else." Then she took off her pants, before adding, "I've taken all the time I can."

Sarah was down to her underwear. Then she fished behind her back to undo her bra. Tom spoke, "Sarah, you don't have to..."

He didn't finish. Perhaps a part of him realized that Sarah needed this, to reconnect with him in this way. So he waited until she was finished.

Sarah now stood before him in all her glory. "Well?" she asked.

Tom stood up. He got very close to her, then said, "Unless we're being invaded by an army, I'm afraid Conrad will have to do without us for a while."

Sarah grinned.

CHAPTER ELEVEN

CAL WHITTEN WAS LIVING a good life.

Well, at least it was a good life compared to what he had had before. For nine years after he graduated high school, he made a living as a truck driver. Cal originally had hoped for a higher paying job, but as it turned out, just about every big business needed one of their goods or products shipped somewhere, across town, to another city, across the state, or even next door to somewhere like South Dakota or Kansas.

The EMP blast from the sun changed all that. Cal's delivery truck was turned into a stationary hulk of metal that couldn't go anywhere. And that was the end of Cal's career as a truck driver. It was almost the end of his life as well. With electronics shot to Hell, the world suddenly fell into chaos, and Cal had to find jobs that would pay in food or water.

Derrick Wellinger was one man offering such jobs, only he promised much more than anyone else was boasting. All Cal Whitten had to do was storm another guy's property and take it from him, with the help of a small cabal of other men.

Unfortunately, the siege didn't work out well. Men all around Cal were felled. Whoever was living on Conrad Drake's ranch didn't take kindly to the intrusion. Cal resented Derrick for not telling them they'd be outclassed like that. Fortunately, Conrad or one of his cohorts took care of the problem – they killed Derrick.

Cal rubbed his greasy moustache with the back of his hand as he looked around the living room, the room that was once Derrick's. It turned out to be a nice bit of compensation for nearly getting his ass blown away.

The soft thumps of a wooden cane drew Cal's attention. Kendall was hobbling inside the room, using a cane to help himself along. His leg still was wrapped in a dull white bandage just under his knee. Kendall was one of Cal's partners in the ranch siege, but he didn't fare so well, having taken a shot in the arm Kendall managed to patch up the wound, but the bullet remained in his body. The once young man started looking gaunt and sickly, and the fact that he was stupid enough to be shot again, this time for trying to steal crops, didn't help. Cal agreed to let Kendall stay in the house in exchange for labor, but at this rate Kendall was sure to kick off, either from lead poisoning or getting killed in another stupid run at Hooper City's crops.

"Did you finish drawing the well?" Cal asked.

"Yeah." Kendall frowned, but then again, the man's face seemed frozen in the same bitter expression since he had arrived here. The man obviously had a lot to complain about nowadays. "Damn near killed me to do it."

Cal stared at Kendall's leg. "Maybe if you weren't so damn stupid to go after Hooper City's storehouse with just one partner at your side, you wouldn't have been shot in the leg."

Kendall glared at Cal. "If you'd have helped me with Derrick's firepower, we'd have made a clean haul."

"And risk my ass?" Cal chuckled. "This farm's got enough for me to live on. I don't need to go out stealing."

"Well, if you had given me more of a provision, I wouldn't have to." Kendall then cried out in pain. "Son of a bitch!" He clutched his arm. "Damn thing always flares up when I jerk it."

Before Cal could retort, or make a comment that would pour more salt in Kendall's wounds, there was a knock at the front door. "Get that," Cal said.

Kendall glared at Cal, but turned and obeyed him, hobbling over to the front door. Then he looked through the keyhole. "Hey. It's that squirt Lance! Remember him?"

"Yeah, I do. See what he wants. I could use an extra hand." Cal looked at the sickly Kendall again and noted to himself that Lance might end up being Kendall's full replacement. Perhaps Cal was indeed living the good life. Just today, he'd get a healthy ranch hand to replace the one with one foot in the grave. He chuckled to himself.

Kendall opened the front door, revealing Lance. Then, a second figure stepped into view, pushing Lance out of the way into the living room, walking immediately into Kendall's face.

"Sorry, friend," Blake said. "Hate to be so upfront, but I'm mighty, mighty pissed and I have questions that need answering."

Kendall's eyes widened. "Uh, Cal!" He still didn't move from in front of this stranger, although his slow legs might have had more to do with that than any bravery he possessed.

Cal turned around. "What the hell is this?" He gestured toward Blake and said to Lance, "Hey, who's this?"

"You talk to me first, kid," Blake said to Lance, "Who's the owner of this ranch?"

Lance shook as he pointed to Cal. "That's...that's Cal."

"Oh, so you're Cal." Blake then shoved Kendall aside. It had taken all of Kendall's efforts not to trip and fall and ended up slamming into the wall instead. Blake then marched to the center of the living room, with Vander and Juan right behind him.

"Hate to bother you, sir, but me and my friends here had a run-in with somebody you might know. Conrad Drake. Name ring a bell?"

Cal backed up toward the hallway. "Conrad Drake? The rancher miles down the road? What about him?"

"Lance tells us you tried to seize his land and got your ass kicked for your trouble." Blake turned his head, showing off a red mark on his right cheek. "Well, we share something in common. We want to know who this guy is, how many people he's got at that ranch. Your old boss, Derrick, he gave you all the info, right?"

"I don't know much about him," Cal said, eyeing the three visitors warily. They looked tough enough, even if they didn't seem to be carrying weapons.

"He's a prepper. You know, those guys who prepare to live off the land in case there's a war or society goes to shit. I don't know how many guys he's got. Maybe two or three people were shooting at us during the fight."

"Well, that's not much to go on." Blake then glanced at Lance. "This visit had better be worth our trouble, kid."

Lance snapped his fingers. "Um, what about guns? Derrick piled up a lot of guns for the ranch battle. He's got some in here, I'm sure!"

"What about it, sir?" Blake turned to Cal. "How about joining us and helping us take down Conrad?"

"Maybe you got some scores to settle?" Vander added.

"Revenge. A dish best served cold, right?" Juan chuckled.

Cal backed up a little more into the hall. "Forget it."

"What?" Blake advanced two steps on him. "You don't want to plant that old rancher six feet under? You saw his ranch. Those crops and animals will set you up for life."

"I'm already set up for life," Cal replied. "I was with Derrick for food and shelter and right now I got both. You want to go round two with that lunatic? Go ahead. But me, I want to stay far away from that guy as possible."

"Suit yourself," Juan said with a grin, "But we're taking the guns."

Cal balled up a fist. "That so?"

Vander placed his right fist in his left palm and loudly cracked his knuckles. "We didn't come here to hear 'No' for an answer, buddy. The guns. Now."

————

CAL KEPT an icy stare on the three men. Meanwhile, Lance slunk along the wall near the living room door. Goosebumps popped up over his arms and legs. This looked like it was going to end ugly, and not just because Blake, Vander and Juan together could overpower Cal. Just before they burst in here, Blake revealed he possessed one last pistol. He had hidden it somewhere under the truck before he and the other men left for Conrad's ranch, so Conrad's cohorts had not discovered it. Blake now was concealing it inside his jacket.

"Alright," Cal finally said. "The guns are in back. Follow me."

Cal backed into the hall. Lance waited to see if Blake or Vander would bark at him to follow. He was nervous enough about such a possibility that he almost took a step to join them.

But instead, he held his ground.

Three seconds later, Kendall burst out from a back room, brandishing a firearm. Lance suddenly realized Cal's companion must have crept out of the room during the conversation.

"Cal! Get down!" Kendall shouted.

Cal jumped to the hall floor as Kendall squeezed off a few shots. Lance threw himself flat onto the ground. He heard the bangs, but didn't see where, or who, they hit.

With Lance's face to the floor, he only could hear the commotion to come. Loud, rapid footsteps retreated into the back of the house. There was a lot of shouting. Lance recognized Vander's and Juan's voices, but not Blake's. Nothing hard had hit the floor. Kendall's shots had not dropped any of Blake's party.

The shouts trailed off into the rear section of the house, which quickly gave way to more gunfire, as well as screams and even loud crashes, like furniture being turned over. The fracas didn't spill back into the front of the house. In fact, Lance realized he had been abandoned.

He was totally alone.

And then, in that moment, Lance realized he actually could escape. Yes, he could escape. He could do it. Now.

It was enough to spur Lance to jump to his feet. Then he pulled open the front door and dashed out onto the walkway that trailed from the ranch toward State Road 22 and beyond. The truck was parked on the road shoulder.

"The truck." Lance panted heavily as he dashed for it. He grabbed the driver's side door handle and pulled on it. The door came open. Blake had not seen fit to lock it. After all, they were in the middle of nowhere. Either that, or he still was fuming too much after his humiliating defeat at Conrad's ranch to remember to take such precautions. Lance hoped that haze of anger was enough to help him get out of here.

Now in the driver's seat, Lance checked the ignition. No key. Of course, Blake would have taken it out and kept it on his person. That habit was too ingrained in almost any driver to forget. But there was a spare around here. He recalled Juan discussing spare keys back at his auto shop. One would be hidden somewhere inside.

Lance flipped down the sun visor. Nothing. Then he opened the glove compartment. Just the truck's insurance, which would nowadays be useless, and a small flashlight. Again, no keys.

"C'mon, c'mon, let me find it. I'm so close," he quickly said as he felt under the seat. Blake thought to hide a gun under the truck itself. Couldn't he have found a place for spare keys?

As he raised his hand back up, one of the front windows of the ranch house suddenly popped. A gunshot must have pierced the glass. The fight inside now was headed toward the front door. Lance's heart quickened. Blake or Vander or Juan would notice that he had bailed.

"Dammit!" Lance slapped his face. "Think. Think!" He then looked down at his shoes, spotting a dark foot mat. He reached down and pulled it up.

Lance cheered. The spare keys were there. Quickly, he snatched them and jabbed one of them into the ignition.

"Please, please," he said.

He turned it. The truck started!

But now he had to turn the shift from park to reverse. He fumbled to find the shift lever. He found it. After turning it to reverse, the truck suddenly lurched backward.

"The brake! The brake!" Lance stomped on it,

stopping the truck so suddenly the force slammed him against the seat.

He turned and looked behind him, not wanting oncoming traffic to strike him. Then he remembered the vast majority of cars had been shut down by the EMP. So why the hell was he checking behind him?

Cursing himself, Lance let off the brake and turned the wheel, swerving the vehicle onto the road. Each turn of the wheel, each step on the gas, or the brake, jolted the vehicle. He was horribly out of practice with driving, plus he was weak from weight loss, overwork and malnutrition.

He turned the truck onto the road just as a pane of glass near the front door exploded. Lance screamed. Was Blake or Vander shooting at him?

Go now!

He hit the gas. The truck launched forward, speeding up quickly as sheer terror kept Lance's foot on the gas pedal. Even though he had put miles between himself and Cal's ranch in a span of minutes, Lance couldn't bring himself to slow down. Only when he spotted a curve ahead did Lance slam on the brakes. He stopped the truck so fast his chest slammed into the steering wheel.

He rubbed his chest and stomach. It hurt, but that didn't matter. He was free! Better yet, he had a working truck. He could go anywhere now. He could put as much distance as he could between himself and Davies.

Then Lance glanced at the gas gauge. It was down

to half. His heart sank a little. True, he could drive this truck, but only until it ran out of gas. Once the tank hit zero, he was stuck.

So, he'd need to be smart. He could go somewhere else, but it couldn't be far.

Lance remembered seeing a town on the map near Cal's ranch. Hooper City. It was worth a shot.

CHAPTER TWELVE

SARAH YAWNED as she strolled down the hallway. Conrad, already awake as usual, stood at the entrance to the kitchen and watched her approach, still in her night clothes. "Morning," he said. "Pretty unusual to see the rising sun, huh?"

Sarah turned, revealing her haggard eyes. "I really want to hurt you right now," she said.

Conrad chuckled. "Now, you be careful. You'll have a sidearm in your hands pretty soon. I don't want you to take that sentiment to heart."

Camilla then approached from behind Sarah, already decked out in her outdoor clothing. "Don't worry," she said, "When it comes time, I'll take any bullets for you, Conrad."

Sarah finally smiled a little. "I'd better get some coffee so I actually can be awake when I start shooting." Her smile widened. "For your sake," she said as she pointed to Conrad.

As Sarah shuffled past Conrad on the way to the kitchen, Darber poked his head through the doorway from the living room. "What's going on? I'm hearing talk about bullets and sidearms?"

"Oh, that." Conrad turned to his friend. "Today's Wednesday. I had scheduled some time at the shooting range outside for all of us. We already had three visitors show up to make trouble, so it's time we became better shots. I'm sure more unwanted guests are going to come sooner or later. You're welcome to come with us."

"Sure," Darber said.

———

DARBER WINCED as Liam fired off the gun. "Yeah, we've been doing these little shooting sessions since the second week of Tom and Sarah's arrival," Conrad explained to Darber from behind the range. Sarah, Carla, Liam, Tom and Camilla all leveled firearms at their respective targets. Initially, the group began by cycling magazines in their sidearms. Now Conrad had them shooting off their weapons at stationary targets to get themselves in the right mindset.

"Have you ever had any problems besides the shootout with Derrick Wellinger?" Darber asked.

"I've had to shoot some critters that came close to my property. But I've never had to deal with actual people coming around to start trouble," Conrad replied.

"Damn!" Liam suddenly shouted.

Conrad stepped over to his son. "Easy. Don't get mad while you got a live weapon in your hand."

Liam looked down at his weapon. "That last shot barely got the edge of the target. I don't why, but aiming is a bit of a bitch this morning."

"Relax yourself," Conrad said calmly, "You're too tense. Don't put yourself in a battlefield mentality. Take this time and let the gun become a part of you. You can afford to mess up at this stage. I'm not grading you."

Liam nodded. "Thanks, Dad. I'm sorry."

Conrad studied his son's expression. "You still got the shootout with Derrick on the brain."

Liam shook his head. "It's hard not to imagine those guys over there on that target. If I'd had hit one or two more of them, maybe things would have turned out better." He took a glance to his side where he had taken that shot.

"Those weasels were hard to hit. You did fine. No one could have expected better for someone with almost no gun experience. Now come on, let's loosen up. Don't shoot so quickly. Get your aim down pat." Conrad then looked past Liam. "I see Carla's got it."

Liam looked at Carla's target. All but two of her shots had struck the bull's-eye in the center.

————

CARLA TURNED THE KNOB. *God, this feels good!* Fresh

water poured from the showerhead and quickly washed over her body. The solar energy plus the pipes that drew from the cistern that gathered rainwater worked the shower, though Carla would be careful not to use too much water.

The others didn't mind, though. Carla needed the shower to wash away any lingering lead that she may have been exposed to. It wasn't a perfect solution, but it gave her a chance to practice shooting without risking her child to lead poisoning.

It was the only time when living out here in the countryside had presented much of a burden. But it was a slight one. Otherwise, she had taken well to this new life.

It really is like a fairy tale, she thought. She recalled her conversation with Conrad the first night she had arrived at the homestead. She had said the ranch seemed like a place out of a storybook.

Of course, her life as a neglected child also had prepared her for a life of roughing it. She had learned to fend for herself. She had gone through a number of foster homes in which the adults who lived there cared little for her. So, Carla learned to steal for herself. Sometimes it made the difference of not going hungry.

This ranch is a place for survivors, Carla thought. *I was always one, even before all the lights went out all over the world.*

———

TOM'S HAND slipped as it pushed open the back door. Liam was already on the other side, on the back porch. The younger man pulled the door all the way open, permitting Tom through.

"Thanks." Tom staggered toward the chairs lining the back porch. Conrad already was seated in his favorite chair, a rocker situated near an old round table draped with a light blue tablecloth.

"Heard you groaning from the other side of the ranch," Conrad said.

Tom sat down in the wooden chair across from him. "Just getting used to the new normal. It's the weirdest thing. On Monday I can spring up from bed, ready to go, but by Friday, I'm exhausted. And don't get me started on Sunday." Tom wiped his forehead. "And then Monday it all starts back up again."

"The human body has its cycles." Conrad sank his head back against the wooden top board of the chair. "You start figuring out how your body runs after a while."

Tom rubbed his head. "Well, I think all that shooting today made my body forget it's Wednesday and not Sunday."

Liam looked around the porch. "Where's Mom?"

"She wanted to rest. I guess she hit the end of her cycle, too," Tom said. "Actually, she got a little dizzy. Being around the hot water from canning this afternoon probably got to her. I told her I'd handle security tonight."

"Well, someone's earned brownie points tonight," Conrad said.

Tom chuckled. "And where's your squeeze gone to?"

"Camilla? She wanted to take a shower. Seems she's a bit tired after a long day, too," Conrad replied. "So, it's pretty much just the men here. Ron is checking over Carla before he turns in."

Liam leaned against one of the back porch's white support posts. "Does this mean we get to use foul language?"

"If you hung around Camilla long enough, she could make you blush after a while," Conrad replied.

"Really?" Tom chortled.

Conrad pointed his right forefinger in the air. "You weren't near the goat pen with her after I came back with Ron after not telling her I was going."

Liam took a seat across from Tom and next to his father. "So, she's really staying for good?"

Conrad licked his bottom lip. "Could be. I get the feeling she wants to. After all that happened in Redmond, she's changed a little. Maybe she feels it's time to stop running around the U.S. of A. and finally settle down somewhere."

Tom coughed. "Damn. The air's pretty dry tonight."

"No kidding." Conrad turned his head to the house. Then, he suddenly rose from his seat. "You two stick around here. I'll be right back."

Conrad quickly left before either Tom or Liam could ask why. With Conrad gone, the pair just sat there and stared up at the night sky. The two men were exhausted after a long day, and with Conrad temporarily removed from their presence, the motivation for conversation seemed to leave with him. He always seemed to draw the energy in a room toward him. Without him, Tom and Liam were free to sit back and actually enjoy the quiet.

A short moment later, Conrad strolled up to the table separating the two men. Then he put down a large glass bottle with a red wax seal. "How about we enjoy our men's night with a drink?" He put down three glasses stacked one in each other, then pulled them all apart and placed one near Tom and another by Liam.

Tom looked at the drink label. "Bourbon," he said, "Texas Bourbon. I guess Camilla isn't big on you drinking this?"

"Actually, she'd probably drink up half the bottle. There's a couple of incidents I'd rather not go into," Conrad said as he popped off the seal. Then he poured some into each glass.

Tom snatched up his glass, while Liam just stared at his. Conrad hesitated before picking up his drink. "Something up?" he asked his son.

"I just realized this is the first time my dad ever poured me a real drink before," Liam said.

"I could have poured you one when we were living

together, but I'd probably have been arrested for giving alcohol to a grade school kid," Conrad said as he sat down. "That, and your mom would have killed me instead of just divorcing me." Then he turned to the back door. "In fact, she still might. Damn, I might have messed up by giving her those shooting lessons."

Liam chuckled. "Thanks, Dad. Don't worry, I'm sure she's fine with me drinking now." He picked up his drink and took a swig. Then suddenly he drew back a little as the bourbon hit his taste buds. "Wow. That...that really is good."

"Strong stuff, isn't it?" Conrad laughed.

Tom drank some as well. "Reminds me of the stuff they passed out at a party once in Omaha. Never thought I'd ever taste anything that good again."

The three men downed another batch from their glasses until Liam spoke up again. "So, are we getting the Daily Drake?"

"The what?" Conrad asked.

"You know, the daily report of the ranch," Tom spoke up. "You always take us out here to tell us how the day went. I already know about the shooting part. Anything we miss?"

"Oh, that." Conrad sat back in his chair. "Well, as it so happens, today we crossed an important finish line. Sarah canned enough veggies to last us through the winter. Add in the beans, corn, peas, potatoes, all the rest, and we're sitting pretty."

Tom smiled. "Remarkable. Sarah's almost like a machine with those cans."

Conrad had taken another drink before continuing. "I wondered how'd she take it out here. I always thought a place like this would be her worst nightmare, especially after we parted."

Tom sat back. "Was that all about your family?"

"I think that had a lot to do with it." Conrad scratched his chin. "Of course, she was born and raised in the suburbs. The country can be a strange place to live if you're not used to it. My family didn't exactly give her the best impression." Conrad poured himself more bourbon. "But at the time, I was living in the city. I thought maybe I could give up that life. I think Sarah thought so, too."

"I guess it was just in your blood," Tom said.

"Yeah. I tried growing a garden in the backyard. She didn't understand why." Conrad pointed his thumb behind him. "Just hop in the car and go get some tomatoes if you want them. That's what she would say." He chuckled. "Well, it was just all about doing it myself, getting my hands dirty. It was like if I knew the crop was growing before my eyes, I knew it'd be there for me."

Tom looked at his now empty glass. "Never could picture Sarah worrying about growing a crop in the backyard. If I tried that, she'd probably take me to the doctor's."

Conrad turned to Tom, still holding his glass. "So, how'd you first meet Sarah?"

Tom put his glass on the table. "It was actually online. It was a small chat room on local garage sales. Turned out she was looking for cheap stuff, since she had just moved to Redmond. We talked for about three months before we actually met each other. I asked her to dinner, she said yes, and then...well, my whole life changed after that."

"What about you and Camilla?" Liam asked.

Conrad drank the last bit of bourbon from his glass. "I met Camilla in South Dakota. There was a convention up there, a gun show, ham radios, sports gear, all that stuff. I sort of bumped into Camilla, actually. Wasn't watching where I was going. My head was filled with all kinds of things. At the time I was looking for transmitters. Turns out so was she."

"So, you two hit it off," Tom said.

Conrad picked up his now empty glass and looked into it. "No, we actually kind of sniped at each other. It wasn't a nasty fight or anything like that. As you know, Camilla has a tongue about her, and I wasn't exactly looking to make any lady friends. I probably forgot my manners. That didn't help."

"So, what happened?" Liam asked.

"I got to know her. I learned more about where she was coming from. She was on the road, just staying in a hotel nearby." Conrad turned his glass over and studied it. "We understood each other a lot better after a while. Turns out we both were lonely. When I left, came home, I didn't think I'd see her again. Then a couple of weeks later, she shows up at my front door."

"You did give her your address, right?" Tom asked.

Conrad looked at Tom, but didn't answer the question. Tom didn't press the issue further. Liam on the other hand laughed and said, "I'm sure Dad did."

"Well, it's been a good few years since," Conrad said, "We never had the sun go down on a day when we were still angry with each other."

Tom exhaled loudly. "I almost didn't realize how much Sarah changed my life until I lost her. Worst thing I ever did was hand her over to Marco and his goons."

"But she forgave you, didn't she?" Conrad asked.

Tom nodded. "Most definitely. Did Camilla forgive you for going off by yourself?"

Conrad poured himself a fresh glass. "Probably not." He then drank a big swig of it.

Tom and Liam looked at each other, trying to discern whether Conrad was joking. Finally, the two of them just laughed.

Tom then raised his glass to Conrad's. "Here's to our women."

Conrad clinked Tom's glass. "Here's to them."

———————

HOOPER CITY. The sign resting just off the road was clean, free of vandalism. That was a good indicator for this town.

As Lance drove down the street into the community, he noticed the looks and occasional excited
shouts from pedestrians. But so far, nobody accosted
his vehicle. Nobody was out and about burning down
homes or shooting citizens in the street. This didn't
seem like a town run by mobs or gangsters. Another
good sign.

A middle-aged man in a blue flannel shirt beckoned to him from an upcoming intersection. After
applying the brakes, Lance rolled down the window.
"Hello there." The man sounded friendly. He didn't
greet Lance with a pistol. Yet another good sign. "See
you got working wheels there."

"Yeah." Lance suddenly coughed. His throat was
drier than he realized.

"Easy. You okay?" The man frowned. "You seem
like you've skipped a few meals there. I was just
curious how that truck's running. It's been a week
since we've seen a working vehicle. Are you from
around here?"

"No." Lance coughed again before speaking.
"No, I'm new. Looking for work." He coughed once
more. "Damn. Sorry. I need work, food, a place to
sleep."

"Calm down," the man said, "if you're looking for
provisions and shelter, check out Hooper Feed. Nigel
Crane owns it, and he's one of our leaders." The man
pointed to the intersection. "Take a left there and
keep going for three more blocks. You'll find Hooper
Feed, no problem."

"Thank you." Lance even smiled, to his own surprise. The man simply nodded and backed away.

Lance was amazed that he should be astonished over feeling good, but he quickly understood why. He just had concluded a conversation where no one barked at him or insulted him. Who would have thought common civility could be in such short supply?

———

A SHORT TIME LATER, Lance arrived at Hooper Feed. Nigel Crane and Jeff Clement, an employee and friend of Nigel's, emerged from the store and greeted him. So far, the people of Hooper City seemed pleasant and welcoming, and more importantly, stable. Still, the number of looks Lance got from pedestrians unnerved him. Lance had heard stories of people mobbing automobiles that still were functioning, and he feared he could suffer a similar fate.

"This truck's still running." Jeff looked the vehicle over as Nigel paced in front of Lance in the small lot in front of Hooper Feed. "Pretty old model." Jeff rubbed his balding forehead. "Not too old, but it sounds like it's been refitted."

"Yeah," Lance said, "I mean, I don't know. It's not mine. I, uh, I took it from some guys that were holding me. Imprisoning me."

"Really?" Nigel asked. "Well, you do look banged up. What happened?"

"I was looking for work in Davies. And then..." Lance held off on telling them about how they wanted his help finding Conrad. At least, Lance wouldn't reveal the name. "...they took me out of town in the truck for a job. They tied me up. But they got into a fight with another rancher. I took the truck during the fight." Lance then stumbled. He quickly caught himself. Even talking that much exhausted him.

"Hold on there. You need some water and food in that belly," Nigel said. "You can give us details later."

"Really? I mean, do you need me to work for it? I can. Just..." Lance gasped. "Just tell me your town isn't run by psychos."

Jeff chuckled. "No, I don't think so. Although I don't ask what our council does on Saturday when they're all behind closed doors and we don't see them."

Lance's eyes widened.

"That's a joke, kid. We may have suffered through the apocalypse, but we still can laugh once in a while." Jeff pulled his oversized flannel shirt taut. "Hooper City is run by a city council. It's not much different now then it was when the lights were on. We had to make some adjustments when everything shut down, but we're pulling it together."

"You want to work? We could use extra guards for the crops," Nigel said. "When you get your strength back, you can help us dig the wells. Food production's picking up, but the water supply's a little weak, and if our population starts surging, we may have a problem."

Lance laughed. "I can dig. Yeah, I can do it. Anything."

"You're eager. That's good." Nigel turned to Jeff. "Help out our friend. Reg can give him a place to sleep." Nigel scratched his right cheek as he peered over at Lance again. "Oh, I forgot to ask. Can you handle a firearm?"

The back of Lance's neck tensed up. "Um, yeah." *Damn, why'd you say that?* Lance fumed at himself. Thanks to his horrible time at Conrad's ranch, even thinking about picking up a gun again gave him jitters. He didn't want to jump right back into a situation where he'd need to shoot somebody.

"Good. Like I said, we need guards for the crops. We've had problems with thieves recently. Some of them are gunmen who have been raiding ranches. But I think we got enough men that we can put them out of business, at least in Hooper City." Nigel gently slapped Lance's arm. "Don't worry. I won't put you on the front line right away. Actually, we can use callers, people who sound an alarm when there's trouble. Without any phones, we have to do it the old-fashioned way."

Lance nodded. "Yeah."

Jeff led Lance off to get something to eat. For the first time in ages, he felt as if he finally had escaped danger. This place was warm and welcoming. Perhaps he could settle down here. There was no way Vander,

Blake and Juan could find him in Hooper City. The road that had taken Lance here branched off several times along the way, leading to any number of small towns. Perhaps the three men all were dead, and in any case, it would be tough for any of them to track him down. It's not like GPSes worked any longer.

Maybe the nightmare's finally over, Lance thought.

CHAPTER THIRTEEN

THE FRONT DOOR to the Wellinger house suddenly flew open after being shut for about three days. Several men stepped through, single file, slowly, with guns drawn. Five of them wore masks over their faces. The sixth, however, did not. He was content with his long coat with a big collar and the hat that covered his scalp. Hunter was feared enough by those who knew him, and for those ignorant of his reputation, they would find out soon enough why even the men didn't want to cross him.

The house smelled rotten. Flies buzzed around the living room. Yet, there was no sign of anyone. The room lay empty of any human life.

The men looked in the kitchen. An adult male lay on his belly on the floor, his hand outstretched for the side door. Yet, the limb lay limp on top of a small stepstool that got in the man's way. A trail of dried blood followed his legs toward the entrance to the living room.

One of the men kicked the body over to reveal the face. His eyes were open, his mouth closed. He likely had perished crawling through here. The stomach area of his shirt was dark red, indicating he was either shot or stabbed in the abdomen.

"Blake," Hunter said.

The men exchanged frowns. Clearly, they wouldn't be getting any answers from this guy.

They left the kitchen and proceeded down the hall, but with greater caution. Now that they knew one of their own had been killed, they realized danger still could be lurking around any corner. From here, the rotting smells grew worse. The hallway walls also were riddled with bullet holes. Hunter looked down. Dark powder occasionally appeared near their boots, with the occasional tiny bits of broken metal. A gun battle had taken place.

One of the men pushed open the door to a bedroom. Judging by the size, it was likely this house's master bedroom. The door's parting only assaulted their nostrils further with additional stench. It was not hard to see why. Two adult males lay draped across the bed. Their shirts were coated in dried blood. One of them was a muscle-bound hulk, while the other was much thinner and looked sickly. Yet, each was clutching a nasty-looking hunting knife. The big guy also had a gunshot wound in his right shoulder.

"Vander," Hunter said.

One of Hunter's men pointed to Vander. "Looks like somebody nailed him."

"That didn't kill him. It only slowed him down." Hunter leaned over Vander's opponent. "The gunshot may have evened the odds. These two then killed each other."

"Damn. Never thought anyone would take out Vander," said one of the men behind Hunter.

"But three of them left with that kid, whatever his name was," said a tall, bald-headed man.

The group's attention was drawn to another man, Behr, who dashed into the room. "Hey! I found another guy dead in the backyard. Had another trail of blood behind him just like Blake, but he wasn't one of ours."

"Shit," said the bald-headed man, "If they're all dead, we got nothing."

Behr brushed his oily red moustache. "Yeah, this place is a slaughterhouse."

Just then, a voice shouted from the hall. "Hunter! Hey, I found Juan!"

Hunter quickly pushed his way past Behr to make way into the hallway. "Is he alive?" Hunter shouted back.

"Yeah, but not for much longer. He's screwed up badly. You gotta come quick."

The team filed out of the bedroom and followed the voice to the house's den. The man who called

Hunter beckoned to a thin adult male lying on the floor. The group encircled him.

Juan was practically at death's door. His eyes were half-open and unfocused. Sweat covered his body. His pants were soiled, with the accompanying odor to confirm it. Crumbs dotted his shirt collar and face near his mouth. A rag was wrapped tightly around his right arm. It was soaked with blood, which gave it a brownish color.

Fallon, the man who called in Hunter, gestured to the arm. The skin had turned green around the rag. Juan had been injured, yet survived. However, he did not treat himself for his wounds, or perhaps could not find the necessary medical supplies to bind his wounds and treat possible infections. He likely was too badly hurt to leave the house under his own strength, and the nearest town was hours away on foot. Since the truck Blake, Juan and Vander had driven here was gone, Juan likely was marooned here.

"Juan. Hey, Juan!" Fallon called. "What the hell happened here?"

Juan's eyelids fluttered. "Hey...Fallon...you... bring...the beer?"

"He's out of his damn mind," snapped Behr.

"Juan, what happened?" Fallon raised his voice. "Vander and Blake are dead. We can't find that kid you took along to get Doctor Darber back. The truck isn't here."

"The kid...Lance...he stole...stole truck...stole

truck and fly away." Juan giggled, showing off his dirty teeth.

"Where is the doctor?" This time the question came from Hunter.

"He go somewhere, I don't know." Juan laughed again.

"Where is he?" Hunter roared.

Some of the men stood back, giving Hunter space. Juan, however, was too out of it to be afraid of Hunter any longer. "Lance-y show us on map. He know. I not remember." Juan then coughed. It was a long, dry hack, followed by an elongated sigh. Finally, he said, in a labored whisper, "Hey. When you bring doctor? I don't feel good."

"You damn fool!" Hunter fished out a small switchblade from inside his coat. "We have no time for this. Tell us where the doctor is, or I'll cut out your heart and shove it in your mouth."

Juan didn't answer right away, taking about half a minute before saying, "It's like this..." His words now were slurred. The next few sentences were unintelligible. Then Juan started moaning, which sounded almost like laughter.

That all stopped when the top of Juan's head suddenly burst open. Blood and small bits of skull sped off in many directions.

The men all looked to the doorway. A lone figure in the hall just beyond the doorway clutched a gun with fresh smoke pouring from the barrel. Everyone stood at attention. No one moved an inch.

"There is a town nearby," the shooter said. "We'll renew our search there. Take two hours to ransack this ranch of anything immediately useful to us, then get back to the truck."

"Of course," Hunter said. "Consider it done."

The shooter backed up into the hall. Only then did the men breathe deeply. It was understandable, after all. When in the presence of the leader of the town of Davies, Kurt Marsh, it seemed no one could even breathe without his permission.

———

DARBER PULLED BACK the tongue depressor from Carla's mouth. "And, perfect. No infections, no signs of bacteria, no allergies."

A loud sneeze rang out in the hallway beyond Carla and Liam's room. Darber turned around, as did Conrad, who was standing in the corner by the bed, while Carla giggled. "As opposed to other members of this household," Darber said.

Tom poked his head into the room. He was clutching a tissue over his mouth. "Sorry." Then he blew his nose with a loud honking sound. "God knows what I picked up out there."

"Could be ragweed or pollen. You've been working around the animals without incident for a few weeks, so I doubt you have animal allergies," Darber said.

"Lucky me," Tom said, then blew his nose again.

"Even so, stay clear of animals with long hair for a while and see what happens," Darber said, "Let's see if it helps you recover more quickly."

"Yeah." Sarah then approached Tom and lightly tapped him on the shoulder. "I don't need a night watchman who sneezes all the time."

"It'd be like painting a target on my head," Tom replied. "I sneeze, and the bad guys know where to shoot."

Darber stood up. "Anyway, we're finished here."

Carla jumped up. "Thanks." Then she gave Darber a hug before exiting the room. Tom and Sarah turned and departed down the hall ahead of Carla.

Conrad waited until Carla had left before taking Darber by the shoulder. "Oh, Ron." He pulled Darber a little closer before speaking again, a little more quietly. "I think it's about time we tend to our other piece of business. We've been putting it off for too long."

Darber had taken a brief moment to think about what Conrad was saying. "Oh, right. That piece of business."

———

REGINALD POINTED to the closed overhead door on the big building that overshadowed him and Lance. "We just got finished bringing in the latest haul of crops yesterday. Tomorrow, we're going to start dispensing them around town."

Lance looked down the street. "I wish it wasn't so close to the edge of the city."

"Well, we couldn't help that. This was the best storage facility in the area." Reginald, better known as "Reg" to everyone, looked up at the sign that read *Full Moon Storage*. "I know the location leaves it at some more risk, but we set up two good monitoring stations up that street." Reg turned and gestured to the small store just a few yards up the street. "That's where you'll be staying. It used to be a school supply store before we refitted it for a lookout post. It'll free up Morgan to join us over here."

Lance tugged at his new shirt. In addition to shelter and food, the town had provided him with clean clothing. He swore never to take clean clothing for granted ever again. "So, how is this going to work again?"

"Simple." Reg walked out from the shade of the storage facility, allowing the sun to shine on his ebony skin. "When trouble shows up, you rush out to the old copy center and give the alert. We'll take it from there. We set up a chain of runners from one store to another to spread emergency alerts. Now, the gunshots might stir us up, but we can't take any chances."

Reg then turned, his back to the street. "Also, we got a special cloak inside. It's dark red, like those buildings nearby. Stick it on you. In the dark, it's going to be hard to make you out. Just make sure you don't move too quickly until you know you're out of danger."

"You really think of everything, don't you?" Lance laughed.

"We got some helpful tips from a friend of ours. One of our traders is a survivalist. He pops in every now and then. He gave Nigel and the rest of us some advice once the calamity calmed down."

"Good thing he knew about this stuff, huh?" Lance asked.

"No kidding. I've been in the furniture business for twenty years, but I didn't know jack about how to blend into a city during a crisis. That's the 'gray man' theory." Reg chuckled. "Say, you're feeling better, right?"

Lance stretched his arms. "Yeah."

"How about you take a practice run? Go all the way to the store and back. Don't go nuts. Try jogging first."

Lance sucked in some breath. Then he took off running down the street toward the school supply store.

As soon as Lance reached the store, he heard a sound that made him stop before he made the turn back to Reg. He looked ahead, turning his head to the side to aim his ear in the direction of the noise.

The sound grew louder. Then the pebbles on the asphalt near Lance's shoe shook.

"Lance?" Reg called. "Hey, what's going on? You hear something?" Reg started walking toward Lance, but then he slowed his pace. "Hey, does that sound like…"

"A car! No, a truck!" Lance called back.

A few seconds later, a red truck crossed an intersection up ahead. The truck was hauling a small trailer with several adult males riding on top of it. The vehicle only showed itself for an instant, but that's all Lance needed. He had seen that truck before, on the roads of Davies.

"Shit," Lance whispered.

By now Reg had caught up to Lance. "What is it?"

"Shit," Lance repeated.

"Hey, snap out of it. You're as white as a ghost. Do you know who that was?" Reg asked.

"Um…" Lance's first instinct was to say no, but he had given away too much fear in his body language. Besides, he didn't like the idea of lying to Reg. He had been in such ill company for so long that it made him bottle things up. But now that he had been surrounded by good people for three days, he didn't like the idea of hiding things from them.

Lance finally came up with an answer that seemed to quell all his nagging voices. "They're from Davies," he said.

"Davies?" Reg asked. "That's the town Conrad was talking to Nigel about."

"What?" Lance's mouth dropped open at the mention of the name 'Conrad.'

"Yeah. Conrad Drake. He's the survivalist I told

you about. Turns out he came from Davies not too long ago," Reg said.

Lance's skin grew even colder. *Holy shit, I didn't realize these people knew Conrad!*

"I think we better talk to Nigel," Reg said.

Lance was starting to regret he said anything.

———

"Stop here," Kurt ordered.

Fallon, seated in the driver's seat, complied and applied the brakes. In the passenger seat, Kurt waited as his men disembarked from the truck's back seat, the truck bed, and from the trailer, and finally, for Hunter to open Kurt's door.

Hunter nodded as Kurt stepped past him. The rest of the men gave Kurt a little space. Kurt was aware the scene must come off as odd to any bystanders. If they lived in Davies, they'd understand. Under the ruling hand of Kurt Marsh, Davies had been pacified and its citizens fed. Kurt was more than a town leader, he was their god, with Hunter the high priest.

But Doctor Darber had decided to flee Paradise. In Kurt's view, this was a serious sin indeed.

Kurt Marsh's posse gathered in the street, all of them wearing masks except two men. One of them, Hunter, was fairly short but bundled up under a coat and a hat. Kurt was the only figure who fully exposed his face—or lack of it. Most of his ears were burned clean off, and horrible burns scarred him up to his right eye and up over his scalp. He wore no hat to cover his bald, burned head.

"What do we do?" Behr asked.

"A show of force, perhaps?" Hunter asked, in an oily tone that indicated he'd love to put on a violent display.

"No," Kurt replied. "We question the town. Our presence alone will provoke the fear we need. Besides, I don't want to start a fight before I know where my doctor is. Put a bullet in the wrong man and we lose our lead to Darber."

As the men dispersed, Kurt kept his gaze on his surroundings. This part of town was largely abandoned, with fire-damaged buildings on either side of the street and abandoned businesses. Despite the signs of life Hooper City presented, it was clear no community was spared the ravages of societal breakdown. Some just suffered it worse than others.

In part, it saddened Kurt that he never had run across an unscathed community. However, another part of him revolted at the thought. After all, why did his town suffer when another town was spared such a fate?

Cruel fate, Kurt thought. *Cruel fate stole my family when others lived through this madness. I may be more merciful than Fate, or I may be a hundred times worse.* Kurt enjoyed not choosing. It was his way of getting back at Fate. After all, if his family was murdered at random, perhaps Kurt should adopt the same thinking. He'd be as gentle as a lamb or as ruthless as a wolf when the time came.

"Mister Kurt!" Behr ran up to the truck. "The other truck! We found it! It's on the next street over!"

Kurt Marsh walked into the middle of the street. "Then this is the place we've been looking for. Keep asking questions. My doctor could be anywhere around here."

———

"I JUST GOT BACK from Karl's. They didn't run into trouble. So far, all they're doing is going around asking questions about Doctor Ronald Darber," Jeff said.

Nigel leaned against the wall of his store's office. Lance and Jeff joined him inside. Nigel had dismissed Reg to gather more information about their new "guests." "Same story we've been getting all day," Nigel said, scratching his cheekbone.

"Yeah, but they're still brandishing weapons. There's enough of them to cause a ruckus if they wanted. Nigel, we could end up with a panic. People are getting nervous. They're wearing masks over their faces like a street gang," Jeff said.

Nigel shook his head. "We can't let this go on. It's time we all take our posts. All crop stores are guarded night and day until they beat it. I'm going to go find their leader and have a chat with him." He glanced at Lance. "Okay kid, time to saddle up. We need a big show of men outside, and you're going to be one of them."

"Wait! I got to be outside? I'm not the lookout?" Lance asked.

"That's the deal. You want to work for you supper, now's the time." Lance looked at Jeff. "Give the kid a gun. Hopefully, we don't need to use them, but we can't take any chances."

"No, stop, I can't do this!" Lance waved his hands.

"And why is that?" Nigel frowned. "This is a town where we all do our part. Now, you said you could handle a firearm. Time to handle it."

"But...but...you don't understand. I can't let them see me. They know who I am."

Nigel's frown deepened. "They know you? Okay, did you cause them some trouble?"

"That truck. It's one of theirs. I took it from them. I used to work in Davies, but then I escaped."

"Now, that I didn't know." Nigel gripped the back of his office chair. He might be a man of thin build, but his sunken-in facial features made him look almost ghoulish when the man got angry. "Was there a chance these guys would come looking for you?"

"I didn't think so! Maybe they're not! They're asking about Doctor Darber, right? So, all I got to do is duck inside somewhere until they go away. See?"

Nigel's eyes fixed on Lance. The young man swallowed hard as he realized he wasn't helping himself.

"There's twenty masked men rooting through my city looking for Doctor Darber. Somehow, you're involved. There's a lot you didn't tell me when you showed up with that truck. Now, if you want us to hide you, you better spill it all and spill it quickly. We have dozens of men outside risking their necks for this town, and I'm not going to tolerate a quitter when the going gets tough. And if you're partly to blame for them coming here, I might as well boot you outdoors and let them see if they have any business with you."

Lance nodded. "Okay, okay, I'll tell you."

So, he told Nigel and Jeff about how he ended up in Davies and how he worked for Kurt's men, about when he spotted Conrad on the road, and when he told Vander and the other men about it, and his whole journey out here.

"So, how'd you recognize Conrad?" Nigel asked. "You know him?"

"No, never met him," Lance said quickly. That was the truth. He did, however, run away from Conrad while the homesteader was chucking grenades in his direction.

"Then what's the deal?" Nigel asked. "You seem afraid to even talk about him. Like I said, you need to spill it all."

Lance gulped. "You promise not to, you know, tell him about it. I know he comes around here, so you gotta keep this under wraps."

"Did you do something wrong to him?" Jeff asked.

Lance trembled. "You might say. You've heard of Derrick Wellinger, right?"

"Yeah, a regular wannabe rancher who didn't have the touch for it. Why? You crossed paths with him?" Nigel asked.

"You could say that."

"What do you mean?" Nigel curled his right fingers inward. "Be clear, kid. I'm getting tired of the runaround."

"Derrick wanted to...to steal Conrad's ranch. So, he hired a bunch of men with guns to do it. And I...I tagged along."

Jeff's features tightened. "You helped Derrick shoot up his place?"

"I didn't know there'd be anybody there but him. I figured Derrick would just talk Conrad into leaving. Look, I was on my last legs. It was stupid. I get it. I shouldn't have done it."

"You're damn lucky nobody in that house got killed," Jeff said.

"Really? Well, that's good," Lance said.

"Of course, Conrad's son and his main squeeze, plus the girl who's carrying Conrad's grandchild, all were in there. So, he might have something to say about you shooting at them," Nigel added ominously.

Lance's skin chilled. "Oh, shit," he whispered.

"Nigel!" Reg jogged into the room from a nearby hall. "They're headed this way. The whole mob of them."

Nigel sighed. "Thanks, Reg. I'm headed out there." Then he glared at Lance. "You stay here and hide. Wait until I come back."

Nigel had taken a few steps toward the door before he stopped. Jeff was following, but halted when Nigel refused to walk any farther. "There's another side door outside," Nigel said. "I'm not stupid. I know you could run, but I can't spare a man to guard you. You want to run, that's your business. But if you got any sense of personal responsibility in your guts, you'll stick around, because you still owe a debt to somebody."

Then Nigel turned and left, taking Reg and Jeff with him.

Lance poked his head out the door. Sure enough, the side door lay a few steps down the hall, with no obvious locks. A quick escape seemed easy.

Why not run? He didn't owe anybody anything.

He ought to leave this place. He should skip this town, get away while he still could.

Instead, he didn't move from the office.

CHAPTER FOURTEEN

Nigel tried keeping a straight face as he approached the posse, to avoid betraying any fear or apprehension. The odds, though, looked a little grim. Ten men backed up Nigel, but twenty stood in the shadow of Kurt Marsh.

"Welcome to Hooper City," Nigel said, in a neutral tone. "What can we do for you?"

Hunter pointed to the truck that sat in front of Hooper Feed. Nigel had allowed it to be parked there. He had instructed Lance not to drive it around town, since it should be used for emergencies only. Lance eagerly had agreed. Now Nigel wished he had had the foresight to move it to someplace secure where it could not be seen. "Where is the driver of that truck?" Hunter asked, "Who came here?"

"We don't know. Truck's been abandoned for days. Whoever drove it here is long gone," Nigel said. "You've had time to ask around. I'm sure nobody else knows anything. Perhaps your man just went AWOL."

"If you're lying to us, the consequences won't be pretty. The Phoenix will set your town ablaze," Hunter said.

"Hey, if you want the truck back, it's all yours." Nigel pointed to the vehicle. "We don't have a reason to lie to you. We're just trying to put our town back on its feet, to the extent we can."

"You had better—" Hunter began.

But this time Kurt spoke up, cutting him off. "Search the truck," he said.

Five of his men hurried to the vehicle. One of them possessed a spare set of keys, using it to open up the truck's driver side door. The men did a quick examination, pulling open the glove compartment, looking in and under the seats, and flipping down the sun visors.

One of them held up a folded map. Kurt and Hunter quickly approached as the man unfolded it against the side of the truck. Kurt pointed to the circled spot off State Road 22. "There. It says, 'Conrad Drake.' This must be where my doctor is." Kurt then turned to Nigel. "This man, Conrad, does he come around here?"

"Not often," Nigel replied. "What's your beef with him?"

"He took my doctor. I want him back. Will he come here soon?" Kurt asked.

"I don't know," Nigel said. "And I don't think he'll

be so willing to show his face if he spots you with all your men and guns looking to blow his ass away."

"It doesn't matter," Kurt said. "We know where he is."

"You intend to negotiate peacefully for your doctor's return?" Nigel asked.

A few of Kurt's men laughed under their masks. Even Kurt managed a slight, crooked smile.

"We are very good at negotiating. And, you know, I always get what I want. Now, there's still the matter of this truck's driver. He's one of my own, and no one deserts me. So, I expect compensation for him, or Hunter here will light the first match."

"Wait." Nigel raised his hand. "How about some crops and we'll call it even?"

"Not good enough," Hunter said. "A few potatoes won't equal the price of a worker."

Nigel swallowed. "Alright. Then how about gasoline? We have some. Not a lot, about three cans. You know that gas isn't exactly common anymore, and you need it to run those two trucks. You've probably used up a lot in your search."

Kurt's smile lifted his lip to show off his mangled teeth. "You are a shrewd negotiator. Very well. Your gasoline..." Then he wiggled his finger. Six men parted from the group. "Your gas, as well as your motor oils, truck grease, and free meals on the house until we depart tomorrow."

"So be it," Nigel said.

———

NIGEL THRUST THE DOOR OPEN, scaring the wits out of Lance. Nigel then pointed to the young man. "You, go with Reg. We're putting a lot at risk to protect your ass, so you're going to work it off helping us. These bastards want food and supplies. You can help us behind the scenes."

Lance stumbled up. "Right, right."

Nigel shook his head. "We probably can delay them for a day, but with those trucks they can drive straight over to Conrad's. I probably have just enough time to get over there and warn him."

"Wait!" Lance held up a hand. "Are you going to tell him about me?"

"Easy. He doesn't need to know about you, not yet anyway. I'm just telling him about Kurt. Like I said, I'm protecting you. That includes Kurt and Conrad."

Lance nodded. "Thanks."

"Don't mention it. Show me gratitude by staying here and helping us." Nigel turned to the door. "Maybe someday you'll become the kind of man who won't shoot at another for his supper."

———

THE TABLE before Doctor Darber was lined with his tools. Behind him, Conrad sat on his bed with his shirt stripped off. The door to Conrad's bedroom was shut.

"Alright," Darber said, turning around, "Describe the pain for me."

Conrad pointed to his right arm. "It started up the arm. It's not a sharp pain. It's just an ache. I feel it after I do some work. It seems to be getting a little worse all the time."

"Hold up your arm," Darber said.

Conrad obeyed. Darber then felt along his muscles, all the way up to Conrad's shoulder. "You haven't hit or struck this arm recently, have you?"

"No," Conrad said.

"Years ago? Perhaps an old injury you can recall?" Darber asked.

"Nothing so major. I didn't even break this arm," Conrad replied.

Darber studied Conrad's arm further. "If it's not an old injury that's bothering you, you might be suffering from an onset of arthritis. It's natural to start feeling pains at your age. It also could be a sign of vitamin deficiency."

Conrad raised an eyebrow. "Good Lord, Doctor. I pretty much memorized all the vitamin intakes out there. I even bought up a bunch of vitamin supplements before the solar event hit us."

"Why does that not surprise me?" Darber chuckled. "I imagine with your farm, you have some of the healthiest food out here."

"Organically-raised goats, chickens and sheep, Doc. I don't inject any of my animals with chemicals or anything," Conrad said.

The doctor turned around. "Well, there's only one way to be sure." He removed a cloth, uncovering a syringe. "Now, it's not quite the full blood test I could give you if I had a working hospital at my disposal, but with my microscopes handy I can look for some obvious ailments."

As Darber pulled on a pair of plastic gloves, Conrad asked, "You don't suspect anything, do you?"

Darber flexed his fingers. "Just the usuals. Better to rule out anything obvious. Oh, and one more thing." The doctor reached for a small plastic cup with a green cap. "I trust you've drank something this morning?"

Conrad looked at the cup, then to Darber. "You're not going to ask for my stool next, are you?"

"If you volunteer, I won't object," Darber replied, with a deadpan expression.

————

THE NEXT DAY, Conrad pushed aside the curtain to reveal the view of his ranch. The sun had begun rising. In another hour, it would fully ascend from the horizon, and the day's work would begin.

He scratched his chin. Sleep never came easy for him except after periods of great exhaustion. He was one of the last people to go to sleep and the first to awaken. Even now, with multiple people under his roof, Conrad never could sleep in longer than usual.

A slight sunbeam hit the apple tree under which

Conrad's father lay buried. It reminded Conrad that he never fully buried the past. This ranch was the most stable home Conrad ever had known, yet even still, he couldn't fully trust it. Stability was a foreign concept to him. His childhood home under the rule of James Bradford Drake never had been stable. It was a household of competition and strife. Conrad learned while very young to grab for whatever stability he could reach out for. That lesson was burned into him and lasted for decade after decade.

Too late to teach an old dog new tricks, Conrad thought. He might never know peace. At least, not until his health started to falter. By then, he'd have no choice but to step down from his rigorous life. Liam would have to take over the ranch and be its chief protector and the enforcer of its rules.

He stared at the tree again. Old age and health ailments had robbed his father of his fury. Nature was the great equalizer. It brought everything to an end sooner or later.

As he took a short walk down the hall toward the kitchen, he heard a soft crunching sound. Curious, he stepped to the nearest window, one over his kitchen sink and looked outside to his animal pens. Some of his goats and sheep milled about, with one or two taking a soft step that produced no noise. Other animals laid on the grass, not aroused from sleep yet. Conrad figured it could be a deer approaching his property line, but no deer were in sight.

Yet the sounds not only continued, they grew a

little louder. With his curiosity turning into irritation, Conrad hurried to the window by the front door and peered through a gap in the curtains. Three tall shapes strode along the road, approaching the driveway that led to Conrad's front porch. The dim light, plus the fence and tall weeds by the road, made it impossible to discern who they were, or even how many people were approaching.

No wonder Conrad never trusted the seeming stability around him. Anything—or anyone—could come along and take it in an instant.

Calmly, without alarm, Conrad headed back into the hallway.

———

NIGEL'S BOOT crunched on the gravel road. The man was so tired he didn't raise his eyes to the home. So, when he saw another pair of boots on the ground several feet away, he jumped in surprise. The two friends he had brought along—Jeff and Whitney—acted no differently.

"Morning, Conrad," Nigel said, out of breath.

Conrad stood in front of them, a handgun in a holster on his belt with an additional shotgun in his hands. "Morning, Nigel."

"I hope you're on a morning hunt," Jeff said.

"Well, it's a different era. Can't be sneaking up on a man's property during daybreak. Could get your asses blown away, especially by a doddering old blind man like me."

"Doddering old blind man, huh?" Nigel asked, "Well, if you're so blind then we should be the safest men to stare down a gun barrel, since you probably couldn't hit the side of your own barn."

Conrad chuckled. "You got me there." He lowered his weapon. "So, what brings you all out here so early? Oh, right, I guess you snuck over here in the dark of night to get the jars. Didn't want thieves to see you."

Whitney coughed. He then shook his head, shaking his long, white hair. "Well, we wish it was only that bad."

Conrad raised an eyebrow. "That so?"

Jeff sighed. "We got big trouble in Hooper City."

"Two trucks arrived in town yesterday. I mean actual, honest-to-God driving trucks," Nigel said. "They were packed with about twenty men."

"Did they make trouble?" Conrad asked.

"Almost. They were asking questions about Doctor Darber. Someone came into town a few days ago driving a pickup truck. Turned out he was working for Kurt Marsh and fled from his men. We gave him sanctuary, didn't rat him out. But Kurt's men picked up the trail and found the truck." Nigel shook his head. "They found a map inside with your ranch circled with a pen. They know where you are."

Conrad nodded. "So, they got a bead on me."

"I'm sorry I didn't search the truck before they

showed up," Nigel said. "I didn't have any inkling there would be this kind of trouble."

"Sounds like your friend didn't either," Conrad said, with a low growl pouring from his throat.

"Yeah, well, I guess it was his mistake. But he was pretty badly shook up from the experience. He was very thin when he came to us, was badly nourished. I think he was abused pretty bad. Probably wasn't in any shape to tell us about the map," Nigel said.

"I can understand that," Conrad said. "So, why isn't he here now? If he's got trucks, he can show up here pretty quickly," Conrad said.

Nigel shook his head. "Conrad, we're talking about twenty men with a lot of firepower. You may want to think about..." The middle-aged man shrank back a little. He knew this wouldn't be easy to say. "Well, you probably should think about running and hiding."

Conrad's eyes widened, not all the way, but enough to show what he was thinking. Nigel's suggestion had lit a fire in him. "Twenty men, you say? I'll consider myself flattered that they're throwing that many men at me."

"But you can't seriously be thinking of staying there?" Jeff quickly asked. "You're a sitting duck. Think about what happened with just seven men under Derrick. This is bigger shit."

"I wasn't at my ranch when Derrick came gunning for me. This is different. Now I know they're coming," Conrad replied.

"But you'll be outgunned by God knows how much!" Whitney added.

Conrad folded his arms. "And what do you think I have, dear friends?"

Nigel shook his head. "Look, I know you've spent years getting ready for the worst, but..." His voice trailed off.

"But what? What do you think the worst is? When authority breaks down, anything, and I mean anything, could happen. I'm not talking about just a shootout with a few desperate men. I'm talking about guerilla warfare. Using the lay of the land to your advantage. Making the enemy come to you, and then springing a few surprises on them."

Nigel didn't respond. Conrad continued. "I never trusted the world, Nigel. From when I was a boy, I learned to depend on myself. I had to be quicker and smarter than my brothers, and sometimes my own daddy. I've carried that belief all the way to the present, and I'll carry it to my grave. I know you're concerned, but believe me when I tell you I can handle whatever sons of bitches come for me."

Nigel bowed his head. "Alright. I don't know what I can do for you, but I'll do my best."

Conrad waved his hand. "No. Don't put yourself out for me. This fire's coming for me. Don't get involved."

CHAPTER FIFTEEN

CONRAD PUSHED OPEN the basement door, exposing the downstairs room to the soft candlelight in his hand. He didn't like coming down here. Of course, it wasn't because of any problems he had setting up this armory. To the contrary, he was quite proud of the storage racks and chests he had placed here. He also was pleased with the sanctuary room he had set up at the far end of the basement. With its hard metal door and biometric locking system, it would be impossible for any intruders to break through unless they had a tank or a bomb. Even in these insane times, Conrad doubted anyone coming for him would lob a bomb onto his house.

He glanced at the chest before him. No, the reason he disliked this room was because of what it did to him. It was a place that housed tools for killing. These weapons motivated Conrad to think dark thoughts. He never wanted to go there. But men with a mind for violence would be beating a path to his door. It would take another man of violence to stop them.

I've never had to live with killing so many, he thought. Before, during the rescue mission in Redmond, he had shot and killed men who held his ex-wife captive. Yet he lost little sleep over it. Perhaps the events occurred so suddenly that Conrad couldn't imprint them into his memory.

It would be different this time. He had time to think, to plan, to prepare, and finally, to act. Those steps would be impossible to forget.

I'll be whatever I have to be to save my family. I'll be a father. I'll be a hard driving boss. If I must, I'll be cunning, ruthless, and without mercy.

"Mister Conrad?"

Conrad turned his head. Carla was standing at the top of the stairs. He probably should have closed the door, but he was so wrapped up in his own thoughts he didn't even consider his privacy.

"Someone's up nice and early," Conrad said. "I thought I told Liam to let you sleep in."

Carla laughed. "I think Liam crashed into bed before he could tell me that. So, I escaped, and then I noticed your basement door was open."

Conrad turned around as Carla descended the steps. "Actually, it's good you're here. Remember I showed you the sanctuary room?" By now Carla had joined him. "I think it's time I gave you a look at the supply bins, to make sure you know how to access them."

Conrad stepped over to the vault door. There was a keypad right next to the door handle. "Okay, here's hoping I remember the pin code." Then he rapidly punched in a seven-digit sequence of numbers. "Well, what do you know? Mind still works well after all these years."

Then he turned to a small glass pane and pressed his thumb into it. "And a little thumbprint to confirm that, yes, Conrad Drake wants in." Finally, he took hold of the handle and turned it, opening up the vault door. The rancher turned and gestured to the opening. "Ladies first."

Carla obliged, stepping past Conrad, who followed shortly on her heels.

Conrad pointed to the containers around them. "You could last for years if you had to, though it might make you a bit stir crazy. I don't think you'll need to worry about staying in here that long. Absent a nuclear war, I think you could outlast just about anything inside this beauty."

Carla brushed the side of her hip as she watched Conrad. "You're thinking of putting me in here soon, aren't you?"

Conrad turned. "What makes you say that?"

"You're down here, loading up on guns and whatever other cool blow 'em up stuff you stored away, and now you're showing me the bins and things you showed me the first time around." Carla raised an eyebrow. "You don't remember that, do you?"

Conrad sucked in a deep breath. "You got a mind like a steel trap."

Carla rubbed her fingers together. "What's going on?"

"Trouble's coming," Conrad replied.

"Yeah, I know. But is it coming tomorrow, next week?" Carla crossed her arms against her chest. "Did someone tip you off?"

Conrad flexed the fingers of his right hand. "Nigel. He came early and gave me the lowdown. Kurt knows Ron's here. Nigel's bought us time, but not a lot. I got to make plans, and one of them includes sticking you in here until the storm's over."

"I'm glad you decided to ask me nicely." Carla unfolded her arms.

Conrad stepped out of the vault. "It's not about asking. You're carrying..."

"...the future of the world. I know, I know. I got to stay alive and protect my baby. But who's going to protect the man I love?" Carla followed him, stomping the floor loudly as she caught up to Conrad. "In case you don't remember, I got through the last time without a scratch, while he ended up with a nice hole blown in his side. I saved his life."

"This time it's different. The odds are worse, and they're packing even bigger heat. First time it was just a couple of devils showing up at our porch. This time it's Hell itself, led by Beelzebub."

"Well, since you put it that way, why don't we all go hide in there!" Carla asked with obvious sarcasm.

Conrad turned and smiled. "Don't worry. Like I said, it's different this time."

"Why?" Carla asked.

The old man turned to his chest. "Because I know they're coming."

———

CONRAD GLANCED at the map on his workbench as he put the finishing touches on his little "surprise." The small metal casing lay open, and Conrad just had finished placing the small metal trigger inside. *This little baby is small, but it will pack a nasty punch*, he thought.

He was so deep in thought that when Sarah and Camilla surrounded him on either side, he jolted.

"Good Lord, ladies, why don't you just blow an airhorn in my ear? It'll get my attention faster," Conrad asked with a grumble as he pushed aside his tools.

Sarah glanced behind Conrad's back. "I told you he wouldn't hear an elephant tap dancing behind him if he was wrapped up in his work."

"Don't I know it," Camilla said.

Conrad shut the metal casing tight. "Is there something I can help you two with?" he asked gruffly.

"Maybe there's something we can help you with," Camilla said. "You didn't show up outside at all this morning. When Conrad's gone to ground, he's up to something big."

Sarah folded her arms. "So, we thought we'd check up on you."

"Wonderful. Now I have two women to nag me," Conrad said.

"Conrad, this isn't funny. Carla came by and told us Nigel saw you this morning," Camilla said.

"And you wanted to put her down in the sanctuary room until this was over," Sarah added.

"I was going to inform everyone after lunch, but I had to get this in the hopper before then." Conrad held out his hand. "I have to work fast. Don't worry, it's nothing you two need to worry about. By the time all this is sorted out, Kurt and his men won't be much of a problem."

"So, why not let us help you?" Sarah asked.

"No kidding. You know I can handle anything with a sighting scope and a trigger," Camilla said.

Conrad sighed. "Believe me, Camilla, I know."

Camilla let a hand drop along her right hip. "Then what's eating at you?"

Conrad was trapped between his former and current lovers. He bristled. Confiding in anyone never came easy to him, even when he was married. In fact, it may very well have cost him his marriage.

"I have to make some important decisions," Conrad said. "This is going to be a big fight, probably an ugly one. The odds, on paper, don't look good. Now, we do have the shelter down in the basement. It can handle just about anything Kurt and his goon squad could throw at us. Anyone who stays in there likely will come out of this. But now I have to determine who goes in there."

"Carla said you wanted to put her in there. Are you thinking of putting us in there?" Sarah asked.

Conrad chuckled. "Ideally, I'd stuff all of you in that room and bag the bastards myself. But I know you'd never go along with it, plus I do need help." He shook his head. "But there's no way I can do this without knowing the family's going to survive."

Sarah held her right arm. "Liam and Carla. They both have to go in there."

"Good luck getting them to do it," Camilla said. "Liam's not going to leave his dad's side, and Carla isn't going to leave Liam's."

"You're right about that," Conrad said. "And the fact is, the more hands we have on the triggers, the better our chances are. I'm just not sure how to solve this."

"Let's bring Tom and Liam into this," Sarah said. "The more heads, the better."

Conrad nodded. "That's good. Yeah, let's do it."

Sarah departed the den. Camilla, however, stayed at Conrad's side. "Baby steps," she said after a brief moment.

"Excuse me?" Conrad asked.

"Opening up and trusting people with your problems," Camilla replied. "You're taking baby steps, but it's helping."

"I'm just trying to protect all of us," Conrad said. "If I can't make the hard decisions, who can?"

"I think you're scared to let other people see what you're doing," Camilla said. "Or should I call you, 'Shane?'" Conrad frowned, but Camilla pushed on. "Yeah, Sarah mentioned you were talking about that movie."

Conrad stifled a cough. "Glad to hear she's exchanging notes with you."

"Conrad, c'mon. What's really eating at you?" Camilla asked quietly.

Conrad looked back at his little "surprise" on the table. "It's going to get damn ugly real soon. This isn't like in Redmond, where I was shooting at guys who were shooting back at me. Now it's going to be guerilla warfare. To save us, I'm going to need to kill a hell of a lot of people very quickly, and without them seeing it coming."

He braced himself against the table. "Daddy was an angry man at times, but even at his worst, he never killed a single soul. He went to his grave without blood on his hands. I hate to think I could be even worse than he was."

Gently, Camilla wrapped her arm around Conrad's right arm. "Conrad, you never could be as bad or worse than your family. No way in Hell." She looked at the small metal casing on the table. "I don't know what you're going to do, but it's to save all of us. These men would kill us first. I don't have to tell you it's perfectly fine to shoot another man who's out to kill you."

Conrad nodded. "I get that in here," he said, pressing his forefinger against the left side of his head. "In my gut, well, that's a little harder."

"Then let someone else share your burden. Let me help you. Let me be by your side when you do this. We'll both stand together to keep everyone safe."

Conrad looked away as he thought it over. "Together," he repeated softly.

"That's not a foreign word to you, is it? I can bring you a dictionary."

Conrad chuckled once. "I know what it means." He turned to look at her. "Thanks, Cammie. You know, it's amazing how well we get along when our first meeting wasn't all sunshine and roses."

"You stepped on my foot at the West South Dakota Convention, and then walked past me! How the hell could your head be that far up in the clouds?" Camilla asked with a laugh.

"I once stepped into a river and didn't notice until I was three feet under the surface," Conrad said.

"Now you're full of shit!" Camilla playfully punched Conrad on the shoulder.

Conrad took hold of Camilla's wrists. "Well, it's nice to have somebody who knows me so well, and when to call me out when I get too much into myself. You want to share my burden? I couldn't ask for better."

Camilla sank into Conrad's chest. He pulled her close and held her.

———

KEEPING THE CURTAINS CAREFULLY CLOSED, Lance looked out the bathroom window through a small gap between them and the window frame. The scene still was the same. A large group of Kurt's men, about twelve in all, had gathered outside to feast, with all of them seated at a large picnic table. Every now and then Hooper City men would bring them fresh batches of food on plastic trays. Kurt's men were especially eager for meats. To preserve peace, Hooper City's men gave them what they had.

One of the men let out a loud belch. Then he took a can he was drinking from and tossed it into the grass. Apparently, the men from Davies also wanted beer.

It's all worth it just to get them on their way. Lance had overheard one of the men from a nearby store say that. But it seemed as though it was taking forever for them to leave Hooper City.

"Hey, Lance!" Reg called out. Lance turned around. Reg was taking this early evening shift to help with the food dispersal. "Come on, move it. We need to load another round of potatoes and corn. Tammy's handling the rest."

Lance jogged from the window to the restaurant kitchen. He didn't want to be chewed out for slacking off. Nigel had made it clear he owed this town a decent work effort, so Lance toiled hard inside this small restaurant, now devoted to serving the needs of Kurt's men. Even so, he wondered if his cooperation would be enough. Lance still dreaded being kicked out of town when this was over.

I'm a screw-up, he thought.

As he walked toward the table where the potatoes had been dumped from their cloth sack, a loud shout from outside quickly stopped him cold. Lance turned and ran back to the bathroom window. One of the servers, Aaron Sanders, lay on the ground. One of Kurt's men stood over the young man with his fist raised. The brute must have just coldcocked the server, who now was staggering forward toward the building on his hands and knees. Several of the men seated nearby laughed.

"What's the matter?" the brute shouted. "I said get back in there and give me more of your meat!" Then he kicked the man square in the ass, sending him flat on his belly. More laughter erupted.

Lance cringed. The situation outside was worsening, and he felt powerless to stop it. In fact, he had played a part in leading these men here. Lance should have chosen a different town, much farther away. But wouldn't Kurt and his goon squad just have shown up here anyway and harassed the town, even if he hadn't shown up?

"Hey!" Reg's voice called out from through the window. Lance looked back. Reg had left the restaurant and was approaching the wounded man. "Leave him alone. We're out of meat. You ate our whole supply."

The brute hiccupped. Clearly, he had enjoyed his share of the town's beer. Anger was starting to boil up inside Lance. Kurt's men had guzzled on this community's hospitality while caring nothing for the people's efforts. Lance was starting to tire of cowering under thugs.

For a moment, it seemed the brute might ignore Reg. But then he turned around and sucker-punched Reg in the face, sending him tripping over Aaron and rolling down onto the dirt.

And the men laughed again.

"Hey!" Hunter shouted. The man in the coat approached from the street. "Kurt says to pack up. We're retreating to camp just outside the city. The assault will begin tomorrow."

The men pushed aside their chairs and started leaving. However, they still felt too rowdy to let things be. Three of them grabbed the table and pushed it onto its side, emptying all the plates and utensils onto the lawn. One of the men kicked over a nearby garbage can. Another had taken an empty beer bottle and tossed it against the side of the restaurant, shattering the glass into tiny bits.

Fresh sweat dripped down the side of Lance's face. These men might get too rowdy, and Reg and Aaron still were outside, too dazed to climb back on their feet, and no one was coming out to help them.

Lance looked down at himself. He didn't have a gun on his person, and he didn't know where they were stored in this place. No matter. He'd do what he'd have to.

He bolted from the store and ran outside.

The lawn in front of the building was an utter mess. Lance watched out for in the grass. A few stragglers remained, laughing and joking with each other in drunken stupors.

Lance leaned over Reg. "Hey! You okay? Can you get up?"

Reg held the side of his head. "Damn. He hit me good. I'm seeing stars."

Before Lance could check the server, a dark shadow crossed his path. Lance looked up, terrified at the sight.

"Good evening," Kurt said.

Lance gulped. He had seen Kurt several times, but always at a distance. The two never had met personally. It was Blake who personally inducted Lance into Kurt's Davies empire. Would Kurt recognize Lance now?

"We are departing your lovely city," Kurt said blandly. "We thank you for the provisions and shelter." The man then pulled out a glass beer bottle from his coat. Lance's nostrils wretched. That didn't smell at all like beer.

Kurt started dripping some of the liquid on the grass and the overturned table. "Yes, I can say your meats and vegetables were of great quality. You should be commended for making it this far in this new, savage world." Kurt then turned his back to Lance. Lance heard a scratching sound, but couldn't see what Kurt was up to.

"Unfortunately, there's still the matter of you possessing something that is mine. We've taken the truck back, but you still have to pay a penalty. The hospitality was quite nice, but not enough."

Kurt then turned to his side, enough for Lance to see the bottle in his hand, as well as the cloth hanging from it—and the small fire snaking its way up the fabric toward the bottle's mouth.

Then Kurt tossed the bottle into the open doorway of the restaurant.

The bottle broke open and dumped its contents all over the floor. The liquid quickly ignited and created a large fire in the middle of the restaurant. Kurt swiftly pulled out a match, lit it, and tossed it on the gasoline he had dumped onto the grass. Another fire quickly lit up across the table and on the lawn.

Lance's eyes widened in shock, while Kurt calmly turned and walked away. "Consider this mercy. Only a small part of your city will burn, and that's more than anyone deserves in this life anymore."

Kurt then disappeared down the street, but Lance didn't even care to watch him go. He had to get Reg and Aaron out of there, or he'd die. The fire already was spilling out of the restaurant windows, but the smoke was the more immediate threat. Lance grabbed Reg by the arm and pulled him a few feet away. Unfortunately, Lance still was too weak from malnutrition to pull Reg much more.

"Lance, I...I can handle it. Go. Run. Get help," Reg said weakly.

Reg then stumbled to his feet and reached for the server, who now was awake and coughing. Lance was about to do as Reg wanted, until he spotted Tammy inside the restaurant pounding on the storage room window at the right end of the building. She still was in there!

Flames poured out of the front door. There was no way to re-enter the restaurant through there. Lance tried to think. The window was big enough for her to fit through. That might do the trick.

Then he spotted a rock on the ground. "Hey!" Lance ran up to the store. The smoke was gathering and made it hard to breathe, but he refused to back away. "Duck!"

Tammy jumped to the side. Lance gave the rock a good hard throw. It smashed through the window, dead-center, making a large hole in the glass.

The gap wasn't big enough for the woman to climb through, but it was a good start. Lance looked for another rock and found a smaller one. He dashed to the window, and started pounding away at the glass. More than once he missed and cut his hand, but he didn't care.

Finally, he got enough of the glass away that he felt the young woman could crawl through. "Hey!" Lance cried out. "Come on!"

Tammy now was looking dazed, her once-vibrant blue eyes glazing over. Lance reached over and grabbed her, scraping his chest with glass shards in the process. It was painful, but he would not be deterred. He pulled with all his might, and managed to yank her free, but he was so weak that all he did was pull her right on top of him. The pair collapsed onto the grass.

"Over there!" Nigel's voice called. "Quickly, pull them away from there! Get them to fresh air!"

A few pairs of strong hands pulled Tammy and Lance off each other, then dragged each of them away from the burning building. Already, other men were rushing to the fire with water buckets.

Lance coughed all the way to the other side of the street. "Get some clean cloths and bandages. They're both cut up," Nigel said.

As Lance was laid on the ground, he now was face to face with Nigel.

"Hey," Nigel said, "you alright?"

A complaint died on Lance's lips. Instead, the young man said, "Yeah."

"He saved Reg's life, and Tammy's, too," Jeff said. "I got the whole story from Aaron. He went out there and dragged her out of there. Kurt and his men then pulled out. Aaron managed to come to long enough to walk to safety."

Nigel nodded, then turned to Lance. "Well, I guess you really did earn your keep tonight. Good job."

Lance smiled. "Thanks."

The pain lingered. Indeed, it would linger throughout the night and into the next day. But Lance didn't care. For the first time in a long time, he finally felt he was worth something.

CHAPTER SIXTEEN

"HEY! HEY!"

Carla's eyes opened at the sound of Liam's voice. Her boyfriend stood over her. A small tray was unfolded near her bed, holding a plate of fresh eggs, toast, a little ham, and a cup of coffee.

Carla smiled. "Well, thank you." She sat up. "Okay, spill it. What did you do?"

Liam laughed. "What are you talking about? I just thought you'd like a nice breakfast in bed."

Carla just glared at him for a minute, then slid her legs off the bed and onto the floor. "Eat first, drill the real reason out of you later." Laughing, she reached for the food. "I got a little person inside me who's famished."

"The baby?" Liam asked.

"No, my stomach. Oh yeah, I got a baby inside me, too," she said as she raised a fork of eggs to her lips.

Liam watched his beloved eat. Every now and then Carla would look up into his eyes, wondering what he was thinking. A bit of wistfulness was peeking out from his eyes. It was the look of someone who was preparing to go on a journey or perform some kind of dangerous task. Carla had seen it before.

She licked her lips upon swallowing the last bite. "Did your mom cook this?"

"I may have had some help," he admitted.

Then, before Carla could retort, Liam suddenly scooped Carla up in his arms. Carla laughed. "Hey now! It's kind of early for this, don't you think?"

"Oh, I think this is the perfect time." Liam quickly carried Carla down the hall. "Yep, absolutely perfect."

The door to the basement yawned open. Liam turned and started down the stairs. "Hey," Carla asked, "Why are we going into the basement?"

Liam didn't immediately answer. Carla then looked down and spotted the shelter door open, with Doctor Darber inside and Conrad at the door.

"Whoa, what's going on here?" Carla asked.

"Yeah, I guess that breakfast was an apology, but it was for something I was going to do," Liam quickly said as he sped toward the open door. Conrad stepped out just as Liam walked inside the sanctuary room and put Carla down.

"For God's sake, Liam, what the hell?" Carla asked.

Darber took Carla's arm. "It'll only be for about a day. We'll wait here."

"Screw that, you need another shooter, unless you've armed all the goats!" Carla broke loose and rushed to the opening, but Conrad pushed the vault door closed enough to cut her off.

"Sorry, Carla, but this is the way it's got to be," Conrad said.

"Doc, watch over her, and if, you know..." Liam began.

"Your child will be safely delivered. You can bank on it," Darber replied.

Carla wasn't about to accept this. She threw her palm up against the door. "Dammit, don't do this!"

But she had no chance against Conrad's strength. The older man pushed the door shut all the way. Then he pushed the numbers on the keypad. The shelter door locked. With a sigh, he turned and faced his son.

"We had to do it," Liam said.

"Yeah." Conrad agreed, though for one more than one reason. He would have put Liam in there, too, not only to keep him safe, but to keep from seeing what had to happen next. Violence was coming, but if Conrad's plans succeeded, he would be the one to deal out a lot of it.

———

WHAT DO YOU THINK, Kurt? What makes a peaceful man

go wild? Why do you think a regular guy would pick up a gun and shoot someone? Is it over a girl? Money? Pride?

Kurt opened his eyes. The words sounded in his head as a memory from a bygone time. Jimmy Park was just asking a random question. Kurt couldn't recall how the conversation between him and his friend landed on that subject. Why would a peaceful man turn violent? Kurt didn't even remember his reply, if he had given one at all.

As his truck coasted across State Road 22, Kurt sat in the passenger's side of the truck's back seat, deep in thought. He hadn't had time to relax like this in a long time. His thoughts had remained with his men and his hold on Davies. It was so strange suddenly to have nothing to do but sit and wait.

He glimpsed at himself in the rear view mirror, his burns and scars reflecting back at him. Kurt couldn't answer why *any* man would turn violent, but he could say why *he* did. Death and rebirth. Kurt Marsh, family man, suburbanite, died in a blaze of fire. This new man, Kurt the Phoenix, was reborn in his place.

How does a peaceful man turn violent, Jimmy? He learns that's how the world works. He makes killing the tools of his trade.

The biggest irony was that the last time Kurt had laid eyes on Jimmy, Kurt's friend of many years was lying on the street, bleeding from the head, with a handgun dangling from his fingers.

So, Jimmy, what made you pick up a gun and shoot someone? His lifeless friend never answered.

Fallon, driving again, kept his eyes ahead. With the second truck back in Kurt's possession, the trailer no longer was needed to haul the other half of his men, so that group piled into the second truck. The men rode either inside the truck cabs or on the truck beds. Thanks to the truck beds' more solid surface, those men would be able to aim and shoot better when the time came.

Fallon had asked Kurt if he should push on the gas, but Kurt decided against it. Instead, the two trucks would coast down the road, with periodic applications of gas, to preserve their fuel supply. Even with the load they got from Hooper City, gas was a valuable commodity. Besides, it wasn't as if his doctor could go anywhere quickly.

So, it was a surprise when Fallon suddenly hit the brakes.

"Why are we stopping?" Kurt asked.

Fallon put the truck into park. "The first truck's stopped. Something must be up."

Two of the men from the back of the truck climbed out and hurried forward. Kurt waited until a man returned from the first truck and reported in.

"There's a tree blocking the road," he said.

Kurt stepped out of the truck and took a look himself. There, lying a yard in front of his lead truck, was a thick oak tree. The trunk crossed the road from the right to the left, and it was so thick that driving over it was impossible, even for Kurt's trucks.

"Pretty damn convenient," muttered Behr. He walked up to the tree and lightly punched it.

"Hardly a coincidence." Hunter walked up to the break point of the tree. He pointed to the tree bark. It was dark and black, with a faint burning smell wafting from it. "This was done in the last few hours."

Kurt examined the break carefully. "A small explosive. Detonated precisely to topple the tree onto the road."

"Bastards. This was to stop us." Behr curled his fingers into a fist.

Kurt straightened up to his full height. "A cheap and desperate trick. This was the obvious road to his ranch. We'll just go around it. Our trucks can handle the wilderness. There's no way he can stop us from reaching his ranch."

"Doesn't this mean he knows we're coming?" Behr asked.

Kurt started walking toward his truck. "Of course it does. Why does that matter?"

Nobody had the courage to ask Kurt why they should not be concerned.

———

THE TRUCK JOSTLED SLIGHTLY. Kurt barely noticed. His thoughts were centered on the thick trees that surrounded them. For the past hour, the trucks had been climbing a patch of muddy hills. Finding this route presented its challenges. They had driven about thirty minutes, only to be stopped by a deep stream that Kurt refused to risk driving through. Instead, they followed the stream until they discovered a shallow spot. They drove across it and then found themselves on this hilly land.

The land itself challenges me, Kurt thought with some amusement. He enjoyed the thought of the trees and the rivers around here putting up a fight. Back on the road, he even had entertained blowing a hole in that tree with one of his high yield explosives. Yet he quelled his lust for destruction. He would save his weapons for human targets.

This is exciting me, he thought to himself. *I've never been on a hunt like this. I actually may forgive Darber for putting me through this.* Kurt felt the gun under his coat. *That is, if the rewards we reap from this are good enough.*

Kurt raised his left arm. He wore an old wrist-watch, still ticking. It was the only machine he possessed from his old life that hadn't been ravaged when his home burned down or fried by the EMP. The time read two minutes to eleven in the morning. There still was plenty of daylight left. Hunter had suggested taking Conrad's ranch at night, to catch them off-guard. But Kurt rejected the idea. This Conrad Drake sounded like someone who was so paranoid he never would not be on his guard. So, Kurt made it clear this would be an open battle. It couldn't be otherwise.

I wonder about you, Kurt thought. *The fire of the sun transformed this world. Did the sun turn you into a man of war?*

The ground beneath the truck leveled off from an especially steep slope. The sudden leveling of the land raised Kurt's trucks to eye level with State Road 22. A cattle fence stretched forth, running parallel with the road. Kurt reached for the manual window crank and turned it, lowering the glass so he could stick his head out and see better.

He was quite surprised. The number of animals, plus the plentiful land could last for years. It was better than he had imagined, particularly more so than the ranch where Kurt and his men had discovered Blake and the other men. This place would be a great present for his men. And to possess such a ranch out here only could expand Kurt's reach from Davies.

The lead truck performed a sharp turn onto the state road. Kurt's truck quickly followed. Now they had a straight shot to the homestead, which just now was coming into view.

The house was too far away for Kurt and his forces to assault from the road. However, there was an old, small wooden shed that lay a short distance from the house, but close that if the shack suddenly exploded it would rattle the nerves of the people in the house.

Kurt's desire for excitement was reaching its apex.

He wouldn't wait any longer to ring the bell, signaling the fight had begun.

He stood up in his seat and turned around so he was facing backward. Then he pointed to the shed. "Let's shake things up!"

Fallon got the message and slowed down. At the same time, one of the men unzipped a large blue duffle bag. Then he pulled out a rocket-propelled grenade. Kurt quickly ducked back inside and watched the spectacle to come. At this distance, they couldn't miss.

"Open fire!" Kurt shouted.

CHAPTER SEVENTEEN

KURT WATCHED the smoke rise from the remains of the shed. The rocket blast had done its job beautifully. The blast had reduced the small shed down to just a few flaming boards stuck in the ground. As the fire raged, small bits of wood fell and continued burning until they were nothing more than smoldering piles of ash.

I wonder how that little bang shook them up, Kurt thought.

It hadn't seemed to cause any outward panic. Nobody had come out of the house, nobody had tried returning fire, nobody even had tried to flee. Odds are Conrad, Doctor Darber or anyone in the house would be cowering inside.

Maybe not Conrad. Kurt scratched an irritating itch on the side of his burned cheek. If the rumors he heard about this guy were true, Conrad would attempt a counterattack as soon as they got close to the house, with the doctor probably hidden away somewhere deep inside the house, perhaps in a basement or a barricaded room.

So, they wouldn't attempt to surround the house and outshoot Conrad's group in a firefight. Instead, they'd make an assault on the front door. And thanks to these trucks, Kurt's men had their own cover, plus quick mobility if things got rough.

In the lead truck, a few of the men in the bed raised metal plates. These were inspired from the shields of medieval times. Just as the knights of that era would hold up shields to guard against the strike of a sword, these plates would provide some cover from gunshots. Conrad wouldn't find it so easy to take out Kurt's men the way he had taken out Derrick's when they tried seizing his ranch.

I'm going to see what you're made of, Kurt thought with a smile. Then he stuck his head out the window. "Go! Head for the front of the house! Today, this ranch is ours!"

The men in both truck beds laughed and cheered. "Light it up!" one of them cried in the lead truck.

Kurt then sat back inside and spoke to Fallon. "Drive slowly." He didn't know what to expect, but he sure wouldn't walk blindly into it to find out.

Fallon obeyed, allowing the lead truck to gain distance. Soon, the first truck reached a gravel drive that stretched all the way to the homestead. The lead vehicle rolled more slowly, its wheels fighting to gain traction on the gravel surface. Still, it wasn't much of an obstacle. The truck would reach the front of the home within a minute.

Kurt watched as two of his men leveled machine guns at the front door. A quick assault would blow the front door open. Another man clutched a second RPG. This would be used in case Conrad put up a fight. If shots rang out from just behind that front door and the nearby windows, a sudden rocket up their ass would take them out nice and quickly. Doctor or no doctor, Kurt vowed to win this ranch for himself and his followers.

At the halfway point to the house, something clicked loudly under the lead truck.

Kurt didn't have time to fully register the sound when a shrieking explosion blew the truck into the air.

"Son of a bitch!" Fallon turned the wheel hard, spinning the truck a full one hundred and eighty degrees away from a rising fire. Kurt clung to the passenger side door handle for support. Once Fallon had spun the truck around, he hit the gas and ran the vehicle off the gravel driveway, back onto the road.

"Stop! Stop!" Kurt shouted.

Fallon jammed on the brakes. Kurt looked out the window, just in time to see his truck slam down hard onto the ground, a few yards from the gravel drive-way. The truck, now fully aflame, bounced upward once and then hit the ground again, rolling a short way until it stopped near a swaying bushel of tall weeds off the side of the property.

Kurt flung open the door and dashed onto the road. The rest of his men followed, but they stopped short of the gravel road. Their lead truck lay burning, with the bodies of the driver and a few men inside. As Kurt gazed around, he discovered the remains of the men who had been in the truck bed. They were strewn about, most of them not burned at all. The explosion had not killed them. Instead, they died from being flung out of the truck and striking the ground. One of them, ironically, landed flat on top of his metal shield.

"What the hell was that?" Behr asked, "Was that a mine?"

Kurt eyed the crater in the ground where the truck had exploded. "An IED," he said.

"A what?" Behr asked.

"An improvised explosive device," Kurt said, "Something crude, no doubt, but effective." He softly ground his teeth together. "Put in an explosive, hitch it with a switch that's triggered when pressure's applied to it. The weight of a truck, or even a human being, usually will do."

"Who the hell makes things like that?" Behr threw up his hands.

"Someone who will do anything to guard what's his." Kurt kicked a pebble onto the gravel road. "Well, Mister Drake, it seems I understand you now. I'll never take you for a pushover again."

"That tree on the road." Fallon backed up a step,

further onto the road. "That was to lead us here. This was a trap!"

"He's probably got more of those things on the road." Behr pointed to the land around the house. "Maybe he's mined the whole land!"

"No problem." One of them grabbed a stick and tossed it onto the ground. "We'll just throw something in front of us first."

"That won't work," Kurt said. "The IEDs are calibrated for heavier weights. A stick, or even something like a storage chest, won't apply enough pressure to trigger the explosive. Unless you plan to throw another man in front of you, 'testing' for more IEDs is worthless."

The men looked at each other, as if wondering whether Kurt actually suggesting one of them should proceed forward to "scout" out another IED.

"We won't be stopped by this," Hunter said. "What are your orders?"

Kurt hurried back to the truck. "Forget the driveway. It's probably mined all the way to the porch. I don't expect he's mined his land extensively. He couldn't have had that much time to plan after he learned we were coming."

"Listen up!" Kurt then shouted. "Two men are going on this truck. Everyone else is to avoid the driveway and anything that looks like a path. You run your asses to that house. You don't stop until you're inside."

The men nodded, despite obvious looks of fear on

some of their faces. But they all knew that defying Kurt was much worse.

"Oh, and remember something. We're not here to take prisoners, except for the doctor. They're more trouble than they're worth. You find someone, you know what to do."

Suddenly, the sky above cracked with a loud pop. Fallon suddenly lurched backward and fell to the ground. Blood dribbled from his forehead. He never had time to man the truck. His eyes were locked open.

Kurt's fist shook. "Take the house." Then he raised his voice. "Take the house, now!"

Hunter turned to the men, who looked at Fallon's corpse with shock and fear. "You heard the words of the Phoenix! This ranch is ours, and those in it die today!"

The nine men remaining obeyed. Now it was truly do-or-die for all of them.

———

KURT'S MEN broke off into four groups of two, one headed to the front, two charging for the right side of the home, and the last pair aiming for the homestead's back end.

The first pair split up and stepped to opposite sides of the doorframe, each man between the door and a window. No gunshots erupted from either the door or the windows. There was just the front door, and on the porch in front of it lay a mat with "WEL-COME" in big letters.

The man to the left, Tyrone, curled his thumb toward the front door. No sense in waiting. It was time to act.

Tyrone's partner, Kelly, grabbed the front door handle. It was unlocked.

"Shit," Kelly said softly. He pushed the door all the way open.

Again, Tyrone and Kelly flattened themselves against the outside wall. But no bullets greeted them. The pair glanced at the open doorway. Only a closed screen door was there to greet them.

Tyrone had taken the door handle and pushed on it. The screen door opened easily.

"This is crazy, T," Kelly said, "This codger didn't even lock his front door?"

Tyrone crouched down while aiming his gun into the living room. "Yeah, well, he's not fooling me for a damn minute. Get your ass down and get ready to spray bullets."

Kelly followed his partner's lead. Keeping low, the pair crept inside the homestead's living room. The place lay still. Nothing moved between or around the couches, tables, and lamps. The doors leading to the kitchen and hallway were closed.

Before either of them could speak, at least four loud pops rattled the far wall of the living room. Kelly opened his mouth to shout something, but

Tyrone slapped him back. Then he put a finger to his lips.

Kelly leaned next to Tyrone's ear and whispered, "They must have got Lee and Sam on the right side."

"I knew it. This is a trap," Tyrone whispered. "Well, they're not getting us." He pointed to the door to the kitchen. "They're hiding in there. Get your gun ready. We spray them first before they come out and bleed us."

Kelly nodded. "Yeah."

Tyrone crawled on the floor, with Kelly beside him, all the way to the kitchen door. The pair then drew their guns on the kitchen door and fired several shots.

"Ha! Think you're smart shit, aren't ya?" Tyrone then charged through the kitchen door.

There was no one there.

Tyrone looked from side to side. All he and Kelly had done was rip a few holes in the wall and the cupboards above the counter and stove.

"What the hell?" Tyrone yelled. "They got to be here!"

He didn't get the chance to ponder where the home's denizens might be hiding, for two shots quickly ripped through his chest.

"Tyrone!" Kelly shouted as he watched his friend slam hard onto the floor. Kelly then looked up and saw two small holes in the window glass.

"They're outside," he whispered.

———

CONRAD LOWERED HIS SCOPE. "Welcome to my home, assholes," he said under his breath.

So far, the plan was working just as he had hoped. A frontal attack, man to man, was out of the question. With Conrad, Liam, Camilla and Tom, that made four to go up against Kurt and his twenty men. Conrad knew they wouldn't stand a chance, even if they added Carla and Ron Darber to the mix.

Instead, Conrad decided to think like a hunter instead of a soldier. Hunters scout out the land and set traps for their prey. Conrad knew all the routes to his ranch, blocked off the most obvious one with a felled tree, and used it to buy him more time to rig his front yard with IEDs. In an instant, he had cut down his number of enemies by probably half.

The next step was turning Kurt's goal into a trap. They wanted the homestead? Sure. He'd even make it easy to get in. It was the perfect switch from Derrick's siege, when Carla, Liam and Camilla were holed up inside against an outside attacking force. But now Kurt's men were inside, and they didn't have the advantage of knowing the house as well as Camilla did. Conrad laid out where the men were likely to go and planned it all out for his hunting party.

Scratch that, hunting *parties*. Conrad had divided his force in two. Camilla was at his side, from this vantage point south of the house, out in the fields, while Liam, Sarah and Tom were closing in on the house from the home's right side. They would be put in charge of taking out the men who entered through the right side of the home.

"But where's the head of the snake?" Conrad whispered.

He wanted Kurt. Not only did Kurt lead this effort, making him a valuable prize in Conrad's eyes, but bagging him might cause the rest of the men to lose heart and flee. Judging from Darber's description of the man, Kurt should be easy to spot. From this distance it was hard to pick out just one man on the outside. However, now that they were splitting up and filing inside in pairs, it was far easier to tell them apart.

But so far Kurt had not made a move for the homestead. Conrad had not spotted anyone fitting Kurt's description charging toward the house.

"You want to split up?" Camilla asked.

"No. They still could pick us off. We'll move in toward the back porch, let Liam handle the house-cleaning," Conrad replied.

Camilla chuckled. "Housecleaning, huh?"

Conrad took up his rifle and started walking back toward the house. "Guaranteed to flush even the most annoying pests out of your home."

CHAPTER EIGHTEEN

"Carla, you might as well sit back and wait. There's no getting past that lock," Darber said.

Carla had been working on the keypad on the inside of this room for the past few hours. "If I ever believed that, I'd never have gotten a decent meal when I was a kid," she muttered.

"I know you must be upset about this," Darber said. "You want to be out there with them, but I'm sure Conrad and Liam did what they thought was right."

Carla spun around. "No, Doctor, I'm not upset. I'm pissed. There's a difference. Right now, I probably could tear this whole door off with my bare hands, but I don't want to hurt my baby trying."

She scratched her right cheek. Unlike the door on the basement side, the inside of the shelter door did not possess a biometric scan, possibly because it would be unnecessary if you already were inside.

"Okay, I've tried every number I can think of, even Liam's birthday and his favorite number."

"It's time-locked," Darber said. "It'll pop open by tonight regardless of what we do. Conrad didn't want to risk us being trapped in here."

"I am not waiting until tonight to see if the man I love and his family are alive or dead." Carla slammed her fist against the back of the door. "Dammit!" She lowered her head. "I get it. You want to save me and the baby. But Liam, you almost died last time. If I didn't help you then..." She let her head fall against the door.

After a short while, she turned to Darber. "There's got to be another unlocking code. Conrad gave it to you, didn't he?"

"I'm afraid I don't know what you're talking about," Darber said quickly, almost as if he had scripted it.

"You're a terrible liar. Don't worry. I'm not going to pump you for it. You wouldn't tell me anyway."

Carla then looked around the room. The place was equipped with storage shelves holding containers with unlocked lids, which made sense, as there was no point in locking up containers in a survival room. The idea was the supplies would be easily accessible to the shelter occupants while they waited out the hostilities beyond the door.

Okay, Mister Conrad, you either left the unlocking code, or a bunch of unlocking codes, written down in here. You knew you'd have to stuff someone in here without filling them in on everything. Either that, or the door's got a manual override, and there's a paper telling me how to unlock it. Carla licked her lips. *Yeah, I got you figured out. You wouldn't risk someone being trapped in here. You had to put in a way out, something easy.*

She left the door behind. Instead, she opened up the first container. The blue box before her was filled with a bevy of packed food. Carla turned up the lid. The codes likely would be taped underneath a box lid.

Unless he already went through this room and took the numbers out. He could be more paranoid than I thought, Carla thought to herself.

"What are you doing?" Darber asked.

"Oh, just looking around. Maybe find something to eat. I am eating for two, you know," Carla said, with a forced smile.

"Oh!" Darber laughed. "I'm sorry, I should have offered you something for the wait." The doctor rose from his chair. "Sarah packed us some lunches." He bent over and picked up an ice chest that sat beside him. "Some sandwiches, fruits, and some tea."

As Darber sorted through the chest, Carla opened up the next container. Still more sealed food and water. She hurried to the next box. Here, she discovered a piece of paper taped to the inside of the lid, just as she had suspected. The paper displayed a diagram of the door and the nearby wall. An arrow with accompanying text pointed to a panel on the right wall near the door.

"Hot damn!" Carla ripped the paper off. "I knew it!"

Darber froze in place. "Carla, what are you doing?"

But Carla already was racing to the right wall. "There...is..." She talked through her heavy breaths. "...a...manual...override...lever." She flipped open a panel, revealing a red lever embedded in the wall. "...right...here!" She grabbed it and pushed upward.

A loud clicking sound cut through the door. The keypad next to it suddenly went dead. Carla turned around, her face curled in a smile of triumph. "Throw this lever, and it cuts off the power to the lock and puts the door back on manual. One little turn of the handle, and I'm gone."

"Carla, please, don't do this," Darber said.

"Sorry, doctor, but they need me." Carla reached for the handle. "You stay here and enjoy the sandwiches."

A shadow then covered the wall near Carla's hand. She recognized the shape the darkness made. She turned around.

Darber clutched a handgun, pointing it in Carla's direction. "I'm sorry. But I'm afraid you're going to have to remain a guest for a while longer."

————

LIAM NEVER COULD FEEL easy about holding this little spherical metal device in his hand, even though his father assured him it wouldn't explode unless he pulled the pin. It wasn't even a real explosive, but Liam had a hard time putting the words "non-lethal" and "grenade" together. Still, Liam kept a tight hold on the small stun grenade in his hand. It would be perfect, not only to gain the advantage over their enemies, but to disorient them without causing serious damage to the house.

Carla. Damn. He wondered if they should have taken her out of here and had her keep her distance from the battle entirely, but Liam knew she'd never go for that. She wanted to help defend their home. Liam understood all of it. Hell, he owed his life to her. But his dad simply couldn't know if the battle would progress out here. Carla's life could be ended by one stray bullet. On the other hand, down in the sanctuary room, Carla was hidden behind a bullet-proof door.

Once this was over, Liam might find himself hiding from Carla behind that same door.

"She'll forgive you," Tom said softly.

Liam turned to the man next to him. "How do you know what I'm thinking?"

"I recognize that look," Tom replied. "You want some advice after this is over? Come talk to me."

"Sssssh!" Sarah held a finger to her lips. "They'll hear you," she mouthed without making a sound.

True, they now were very close to the house, so close they could hear the voices of the surviving men inside. "I don't know where they are!" one of them shouted. "I searched this damn place and haven't found anybody."

"They're hiding, you dumbshit!" answered a second man.

"Will you all knock it the hell off and help me with Tyrone!" cried a third.

"He's dead, you moron, and you will be, too, if you don't help us out," answered the second man. "They took out Bryce and Luiz, too. They're obviously shooting at us from outside, so get in position and start shooting back."

Liam approached the window. Sarah and Tom raised their rifles. Liam didn't have to say, "Cover me." The couple knew their parts.

One of the men suddenly smashed through the glass window with his rifle. Sarah and Tom quickly opened fire. The man fell back. It was impossible to tell if he was hit, but Liam didn't care. He had his opening.

Liam pulled the pin, then threw the grenade through the gap in the window that the gunman so helpfully had made for him.

"Duck!" Tom shouted.

The three dropped to the dirt. All three knew the room on the other side of the window would be engulfed in a piercing light, accompanied by a loud bang that would be hell on the eyes and ears of the men inside.

————

By now, Conrad and Camilla had closed in on the back of the home. However, a loud pop that whizzed by their heads stopped them dead in their tracks.

"Take cover!" Conrad called out as he leveled his rifle. The two dropped down as Conrad quickly looked for their assailant. The grass in this area was tall enough to obscure them if they crouched down, giving Conrad some time to track down their shooter.

For an instant, a swiftly moving shape crossed his field of vision. The man was running right out into the fields behind Conrad's house, on a route that would take him close to Conrad and Camilla. He wasn't even bothering with the house. He had figured out there were shooters out here and had decided to flush them out. And judging from the man's disfigured face, there was no question who now was hunting them.

"The head of the snake is here," Conrad whispered.

CHAPTER NINETEEN

"You have lost your mind!" Carla pointed a finger at the gun-wielding doctor. "You're not actually going to shoot me to stop me from leaving!"

"Times are desperate," Darber said. "I've stood by and endured the horrors of Kurt. I never resisted. I never fought for anything. That's got to change. I told Conrad I'd help deliver your baby, and your baby will be delivered, safe and sound. So, I suggest you sit and enjoy your mother-in-law's sandwiches."

Carla shook her head. "Doctor Ron, I can't. Liam's out there. Don't you understand?"

"Conrad, Liam, Camilla, they all have things well in hand. They filled me in on their plans. Kurt's men won't make it out of here alive. I have faith in them. I just need to do my part."

"That includes maybe shooting a pregnant woman?" Carla threw up her hands. "That's insane! You're a doctor! You know what a bullet would do to a person, and that includes to somebody who's carrying a baby! You really want to pump me with a metal bullet that could poison my child?"

"Oh, you don't have to worry. This isn't loaded with bullets," Darber said. "It's got a tranquilizer. One shot and you'll get real sleepy. You'll spend the next few hours taking a nice nap. By then, Conrad and company should be finished mopping up Kurt's men."

"That still could hurt my child. You'd never risk shooting me up with chemicals unless my life was in danger," Carla said.

"If I don't take that risk, you and your child may not survive at all," Darber replied.

Carla smiled. After observing his eyes and hand movements , she was now sure about what her doctor was up to. "Doctor Ron," she said gently, "we both know you can't stop me from leaving. You wouldn't shoot me with a bullet or a tranquilizer. That gun's a total fake."

Darber tried firming up his expression. "Are you sure you want to take that chance?"

Carla put her hands on her hips. "Pull the trigger."

Darber quivered. Bingo. She had him nailed.

"If that gun's really got true ammo, shoot it at the wall and convince me." Carla pointed to the wall behind her. "Or the floor. Someplace that won't ricochet. C'mon. Do it."

Darber cleared his throat. "That...that would be a waste of a good dart."

Carla shook her head. "C'mon. The jig is up. Put it down."

The doctor sighed, but he did pull the trigger. But instead of a bullet or a dart, the small pistol jettisoned squirts of water on the floor.

Carla once again smiled in triumph. Darber dropped the gun on the ground. "How did you know?" he asked.

"Like I said, you're a terrible liar," she replied. "When I was little, I was around people who lied a lot, and I could tell what they were thinking. At least you were trying to keep me safe. That squirt gun was cute. Who came up with that idea? Liam? Mister Conrad?"

Darber bit his lip. "I did, actually. I suppose that's fitting. I never stood up to the cretins that had taken over my town and, in the end, the firearm I use is a cheap gag squirt gun. If nothing else, you're a much braver person than I am."

Carla then curled her fingers around the handle and pulled it down. From there, she pushed the vault door open.

Darber closed his eyes. "Carla, are you sure about this?"

"A thousand percent." Carla then backed into the basement. She turned to the arsenal on the wall. "Time to arm up. You stay there."

Carla pulled a rifle with a scope off the wall. But

before she could walk off with it, Darber reached for his own rifle.

"What are you doing?" Carla asked.

Darber looked down at the weapon in his hands. "Conrad always can find another doctor, but he can't replace you. So, where you go, I will follow. Besides, I think it's my time to fight as well."

Carla smiled. "Thanks!" Then she patted the doctor's shoulder. "Sorry. I can't hug you with live ammo in my hand."

Darber laughed. "Well, let's get going, shall we?"

————

It was a furious running battle between Kurt and Conrad along the side of the house. The initial spray of bullets from Kurt had caused Camilla to separate from Conrad while he provided her covering fire. Since then, Conrad and Kurt had exchanged fire as both of them got closer and closer to his home.

Kurt's shots were high, so since Conrad kept his head down, not a single one of them struck him. However, they did ricochet off the metal fence near the house, and each pop rattled Conrad to his insides. He hadn't heard or seen Camilla in the past few minutes, but he was sure she was fine. Camilla had a way of showing up when least expected.

As soon as Conrad rounded the corner to the back porch, he fled toward the posts that held the awning over the porch. The posts weren't very wide, but his table was close to one of them. Together, the two would afford him decent cover. He might squeeze off a few shots that would rattle Kurt and cause the gunman to back off.

Unfortunately, Kurt was just a little quicker. He drew a small handgun, his rifle having been discarded, with an eye for Conrad's upper back.

And then a shot nailed Kurt in the upper shoulder. The gunman fell back against the house and then quickly dropped to the ground. This gave Conrad the time he needed to make it to the post with the table. He drew his weapon in Kurt's direction, but by then Kurt had dove for the ground, ducking behind one of the porch chairs.

Conrad glanced in the direction of his savior. Camilla was hiding in the bushes nearby. Conrad only could make out one of her eyes staring at him from behind the bush. Sure enough, Camilla had surprised Conrad once again.

Conrad and Kurt exchanged another round of gunfire before all went silent again. Conrad peered around the side of the post. No movement. He scooted to the other side of the post. A dark shape behind a nearby chair could be Kurt, but he didn't dare expose himself to check. Odds are Camilla couldn't tell either, or she'd have plugged Kurt by now.

Finally, Kurt spoke up, putting at least a verbal end to the stalemate. "You have great cunning, Mister Drake. I assume you are Conrad Drake."

Conrad peered out very carefully to see if he could follow Kurt's voice. When he still couldn't spot Kurt, Conrad drew back. "And I guess you don't need an introduction. Your looks gave you away."

"I prefer it that way," Kurt said. "Fear is a great motivator. It's served me well."

"It's made you a good tyrant, hasn't it?" Conrad asked.

"We're all rulers of our respective countries, Mister Drake. This is your nation. I'm simply conquering it for my own flag," Kurt replied.

"You and what army? Would that be the army that's lying all over my front yard?" Conrad asked. "Maybe you should find another line of work."

"If you have such weapons at your disposal, that makes this ranch all the more valuable for me when I take them for my own," Kurt said.

"Well, tough breaks, buddy. It's not yours and never will be," Conrad retorted. "Why don't you do the smart thing and get the hell off my property while you're still breathing?"

"You would show mercy?" Kurt asked, as if he was slightly offended by the prospect.

"Call it expediency," Conrad said with a growl. By now he didn't relish the thought of letting this bastard live after he had caused so much damage. Conrad also couldn't be sure Kurt's men hadn't killed anyone from his household yet.

"As gentle as a lamb or as vicious as a wolf. That's the choice, is it not?" Kurt asked. "When the mob torched my home and murdered my family, I saw the fangs of the wolf reaching for me. I had survived but, as you can see, at great cost. Then I ventured to other towns and saw how the people treated others with gentleness. It's a sick joke that some are chosen to be victims and others are not."

Conrad looked out again to try to locating Kurt, but the porch clutter made it almost impossible unless Conrad stood up. "Life's a bitch, Kurt. I know it. I heard the story about your family. You got my condolences. Nobody deserves that. But you causing pain and suffering for other people is not going to balance the scales."

"I don't care about balancing the scales. I don't believe in justice anymore, only strength and personal power. If you possess those, you can command Fate itself. When that happens, the fire never comes for you. Now it's yours to wield yourself."

Conrad gritted his teeth. "You're a deluded son of a bitch. Millions of men over the ages have believed that bullshit, and it's never lasted for any of them. Nature's the great equalizer, Kurt. We're all going to die sooner or later, and when that happens, you're not wielding any kind of power."

"And then what? You stand before God? Is that what you'll tell me?" Kurt asked with dripping sarcasm. "Will you preach to me that God exists?"

"I'll say this. My relationship with the Almighty hadn't been smooth sailing for a while. Sometimes I had sharp words with my maker. But recently, I've decided to try patching things up. Now I've got people who depend on me, so I've got to do the most good for them while I still have time on this Earth. That's the only thing that matters."

"How touching." Again, Kurt sounded disgusted, but Conrad thought he detected a whiff of regret or wistfulness in Kurt's voice. The gunman may have resembled a monster, but he still was a human being, one who had experienced a horrific tragedy. It seemed doubtful he could be reasoned with, but it may not be totally impossible.

And then, Kurt stood up to full height.

"I'm sorry to say, Mister Drake, but compassion and mercy are a foreign thing to me now," Kurt said.

Conrad looked up, and found Kurt standing in the shadow of the porch. The gunman's left hand aimed a gun to the bush where Camilla was hiding.

"In a few seconds, I will shoot one of you. I do not know which one I shall choose. I will be as random as Fate itself. So, now the table is set. You or your ladyfriend will have to kill me before I kill one of you. Perhaps Fate or your god will decide who lives and dies today."

Conrad's heartrate quickened. There was no room for hesitation. He had to expose himself and take out this monster once and for all.

He jumped out from the right side, thinking he might have the best chance to nail Kurt. But as he stood up and got a good look at Kurt in the porch, he found the gunman's right hand already was extended in his direction.

Kurt fired both at the bush and at Conrad.

The whole moment transpired in an instant. Camilla opened fire from the bush. Conrad fired one shot. Kurt squeezed off a shot from both hands.

Kurt, Conrad and Camilla all cried out, with Conrad and Kurt each hitting the ground. Intense pain shot up Conrad's left arm. Kurt had nailed him, but not in any vital organ.

"Camilla!" Conrad shouted. He flexed his fingers of his right hand. He had dropped his gun! "Dammit!" He looked around for the weapon.

He found it near the edge of the porch. He grabbed it, but the pain was seizing him hard. Then he looked up at where Kurt had been standing. The gunman was gone. A trail of blood drops led back around the house.

At the same time, Camilla popped out of the bush, holding her shoulder. "Kurt!" She winced. "We got to stop him!"

CHAPTER TWENTY

LIAM PANTED. His quarry had gotten away. Or perhaps he just was hiding somewhere in the living room?

The bright flash and loud bang from the grenade had successfully disoriented the three men. Liam, Sarah and Tom quickly dashed through the nearby door and took out one of the men. The remaining two broke off into opposite ends of the house. Sarah and Tom took off after the one headed for the den, while Liam pursued the other, who had fled for the living room.

After a brief shooting battle, Liam had lost track of his target. The young Drake kept flat against the hallway wall as he peered into the living room. Kurt's henchman could be hiding behind the couch, or maybe crouched down along the wall.

Wish I had a second flash grenade on me, Liam

thought. Another grenade would smoke out Liam's target, wherever he was.

Liam then turned to the front doorway. The front door lay open while the screen door was closing back into the doorframe. "Of course," Liam mouthed soundlessly. The man obviously wanted to escape.

Liam was inclined to allow the man to escape. Assuming, of course, that Kurt's man did want to flee the property altogether and not just take up a position outside to pelt the house with bullets. So, Liam had to make sure. He rushed to the screen door, then flung it open. The front door remained open, allowing Liam an unobstructed path out to the porch.

No one fired a shot his way. Liam poked his head out, looking to the left and the right.

To the left, he discovered nothing. To the right, he was greeted with a black-gloved fist that flew to his face so quickly Liam had no time to turn his gun on the assailant.

The blow hit Liam hard, sending him slamming into the doorframe. But his assailant wasn't the henchman he was pursuing. Instead, he was accosted by a shorter man dressed in a coat and a hat.

Liam had no time to ponder the change in his opponent, for Hunter was about to throw another punch. Liam ducked and rolled out of the way. Then he realized his hands were free. He had dropped the rifle when Hunter hit him.

Damn! Liam raced to the rifle lying on the deck, and kicked it out of the way before Hunter could grab it. The weapon sailed across the deck and dropped off the side. Hunter turned his full attention on Liam. His hands were empty.

"No gun?" Liam quickly patted the side of his head where Hunter had struck it.

"Unnecessary," Hunter replied as he spread his arms in a fighting stance.

Liam and Hunter circled each other. "Why do I think you just emptied out your ammo already? You guys really are poor shots."

"I give you credit for devising such ruthless tactics. A shame you are not working for us," Hunter said.

"Screw off. I have family to protect, and I wouldn't be caught dead working for shitheads like you," Liam retorted.

"A shame, but no matter. The Phoenix shall burn bright this day," Hunter said.

"What? You're talking about your boss?" Liam asked.

"Indeed. This ranch belongs to him now, and I will deliver it to him over the corpses of all who live here," Hunter replied.

Liam shook his head. "Damn. You're one sick bastard. You sound like you worship the guy."

"Perhaps," Hunter said. "Perhaps in this life, you make your own Heaven or Hell."

Hunter then lunged at Liam. He was quick. Liam only dodged him by an inch. Liam tried throwing another punch, but Hunter jumped away just in time.

Liam might be stronger, but Hunter had greater agility, even with that coat on. Whoever this man was, he evidently had some training in hand-to-hand combat. Liam realized he might be outclassed by this guy if he didn't put him down quickly.

But there seemed to be no chance of that happening. And when Hunter kicked Liam hard in the stomach, Liam's chances seemed to be headed for zero. The pain was so intense Liam couldn't do anything but catch his breath.

Hunter then reached into his coat. The henchman pulled out a small handgun. "I'm afraid you were quite wrong," Hunter said. "I had one more tucked away." Then he aimed his weapon at Liam.

But before Hunter could squeeze the trigger, Carla burst from the front door, wielding a rifle. It was just enough to stop Hunter in his tracks to assess the new threat that emerged before him.

Carla was at the ready, squeezing the trigger three times. One struck the fence close to Hunter's ear. Another impaled Hunter in the upper torso. A third struck the porch, kicking up small shards of wood that hit Hunter in the leg.

Kurt's henchman shouted in pain. Dropping his gun, he quickly fell backward, landing hard on the deck. Liam then turned to see his girlfriend rushing toward him with a rifle. Darber followed, similarly armed.

"Carla!" Liam laughed with relief, but some

outrage bubbled up inside him as well. "What are you doing here?"

"I got bored," Carla replied. Beside her, Darber was looking back and forth up the side of the house with his own rifle in hand. "What's the story?" she asked.

"Most of them are taken out, but we still have maybe one or two left. Kurt chased after Dad. We got to find—"

Suddenly, a shot rang out. With a shout, Carla lurched forward. Only by falling against the front wall of the house did she manage not to slam onto the porch.

"Carla!" Liam screamed.

"No!" Darber ran toward her.

Kurt stood a few feet away on the edge of the porch with a handgun, fresh smoke pouring from the barrel.

The whole scene instantly replayed in Liam's mind. Carla had been shot in the back, somewhere in the back. The bullet did not exit, at least not anywhere that Liam had seen. The shot seemed to be above Carla's abdomen. It did not seem to hit her heart.

Liam could not be sure. He chose to believe it. The one thing he was sure of was that he was going to tear Kurt Marsh's head from his body.

However, Kurt reacted much quicker. He turned the gun around and smashed in Liam's nose with it.

The force dropped Liam to the porch floor like a bag of cement.

Kurt aimed his gun at Liam's face and spoke a word, but Liam could not hear it. The world around him was just a loud hum, and the ground beneath him spun. He could sit up, but that was all. The only other thing he was sure of was that Darber was tending to Carla.

But then a loud shout of "Kurt!" followed by a swiftly moving shadow from the right drew Kurt's attention. Gunfire erupted from somewhere near the porch's right hand side. But Kurt didn't drop.

Then Liam discovered why. Camilla stood there, leaning against the porch banister with a rifle in her hand. But Hunter had jumped in front of Kurt and spread out his arms, giving him the widest possible profile. The lackey had taken every shot for Kurt.

Hunter trembled, but did not fall yet. Instead, Kurt took hold of him before he fell. With so much of Hunter's face covered, no one could see any expression of agony.

"Son of a bitch," Liam whispered.

Kurt gazed at Hunter with widening eyes, as if to ask "Why?"

Hunter spoke something in a croaking voice, but it was unintelligible. The henchman then lost all strength. Kurt allowed Hunter to drop to the ground. He landed in a sitting position, propped against Kurt's legs. Kurt then stepped aside and allowed the man to drop onto his side. Hunter did not breathe again.

Conrad then hobbled into view. "Unbelievable," he said. Kurt just looked down at his feet. The man seemed shocked by what had happened, which sparked some additional irritation in Conrad.

"What's the matter?" Conrad asked. "I thought you preferred to have your men give their lives for you? Is this supposed to be shocking or something?"

"I remembered," Kurt said, "a time past, when I called other men friends." He looked up at Conrad and Camilla. His eyes seemed different now. The brown in his pupils seemed deeper, more focused. "For a brief moment, I thought of Hunter as such a friend."

"You really believe that?" Darber asked. "You think he felt genuine friendship for you? That town was at your feet. Everyone feared you. I don't think there was a soul there who cared for you."

Kurt then groaned. His pant legs were becoming redder. His gunshot wounds were bleeding out, and badly. It was clear he had taken multiple hits back at the porch. Kurt had to spread out his left leg just to brace himself and remain standing.

"That woman. She will live?" Kurt asked Darber.

"A good chance, I hope, though I also have to worry about her unborn baby." Darber narrowed his eyes. "Conrad's grandchild."

Kurt's bottom lip dropped open, before he curled it up in a smile. "I see. So, I've shot a pregnant woman?" Then he turned to Conrad. "So, Mister Conrad, gentle as a lamb or as savage as a wolf? Tell me, would you offer mercy now?"

Conrad's eyes locked on Kurt. "Get Carla inside. Save her life. Save my grandchild," he said, to no one in particular.

Liam, Sarah and Tom helped Darber with Carla, leaving only Camilla outside with Conrad and Kurt.

"So, let's settle this." Kurt raised his gun only slightly. "I wish I could say this would be a fair contest. But, I barely can stand as it is, and my right arm's feeling numb. You would have to go to great effort to save my life. Even with what I've done to you and your family, you might actually try to do it."

Kurt raised his gun, but then turned the barrel upward. "Sadly, as I said before..." Now Kurt's breathing sounded labored. "I can't entertain mercy any longer, not even for myself."

Then he turned the gun to the side of his head and pulled the trigger.

Conrad's eyes fixed on everything that followed, from Kurt's gun dropping from his fingers, to Kurt's whole body dropping down onto the grass. Then he glanced in Camilla's direction. Her eyes were wide with shock.

"I don't get it. Why'd he do it? He didn't want you to take him alive?" Camilla asked.

Conrad hobbled over to Kurt's body. "For a moment, he became human again. I think that was too much for him." He glanced back at Camilla.

"When a monster gets his soul back, it's hard to go back to being a monster."

Clutching her wounded shoulder, Camilla glanced over at Hunter's bullet-riddled body. "I wish I could believe these two were human, but I'll never believe it. Nobody with a conscience could do all this."

Conrad gripped his arm. "Well, only God's going to make that determination now." He turned to the door. "Let's hurry inside or we'll bleed out all over the deck. And we got to help Carla."

As Camilla walked beside Conrad, he cast a brief glance at her. "You saved me back there. You were right about having someone share the burden."

Camilla opened the front door. "You think maybe you'll finally think about the 'm' word?"

Conrad pushed the door all the way open. "Maybe," he said as Camilla walked through the door past him.

————

FIND out what happens in part four available now!

Made in the USA
Las Vegas, NV
27 March 2021

20179172R00135